"A SPLENDID NARRATIVE."   —*Chicago Daily News*

The countless readers of Andr[...]est-selling science-fiction novels, who ha[...] terrific scenes of adventure a[...]ds of fantastic beasts a[...] find that same fascination [...]ng of a similar tale of fantastic adv[...]wn world's romantic past.

HUON OF THE HORN is the story of the young knight, Huon of Bordeaux, who through treachery was banished from the court of the legendary Charlemagne until he could fulfill an almost impossible quest in Babylon. In it courage, swordplay, romance and the magic of medieval witchcraft combine in a novel that will thrill modern readers as much as it did their ancestors in the days of knights, fire-breathing dragons, and damsels in distress.

Huon of the Horn

A tale of that Duke of Bordeaux who came to sorrow at the hands of Charlemagne and yet won the favor of Oberon, the elf king, to his lasting fame and great glory.

Adapted by

ANDRE NORTON

Illustrated by Joe Krush

An Ace Book
Ace Publishing Corporation
1120 Avenue of the Americas
New York, N.Y. 10036

The romance of Huon of Bordeaux is included in the cycle of the Charlemagne Saga although it was apparently compiled at a much later date than were the stories concerning Roland, Ogier and the other and more familiar heroes. Kipling drew upon this legend of the mortal king who ruled in Fairyland in his Puck of Pook's Hill, *but the entire tale of the exiled knight who won his right to return to France by the favor of the Elf King Oberon is not as well known as the other romances of chivalry—perhaps because the best known English translation still remains that made by Sir John Bourchier (Lord Berners) in 1534, the quaint language of which makes difficult reading today. This present adaption is based upon his* Boke of Duke Huon of Burdeux *as it appears in the publications of the Early English Text Society.*

ADVENTURE THE FIRST

I. WHICH TELLETH HOW KING CHARLEMAGNE SUMMONED THE PEERS OF FRANCE

Now it chanced that in those grim and sorrowful days which came to the court and land of France after the death of Roland and the other noble dukes and brave lords who fell with him in that last great battle against the Saracens, King Charlemagne was driven to think much of the future of his realm. And sober and stern were his thoughts because of the evil which might befall his people now that these great heroes were gone from amongst them.

Thus he was moved to summon unto his court all the paramount lords and peers yet living, that he might take council with them concerning France in the days to come. But of the mighty Twelve who had once upheld his throne there was left only the Duke Naymes of Bauyer.

To his counsel would the King ever listen, for Duke Naymes had been comrade-in-arms, shield-mate and cup-brother to those who had gone—Roland and Oliver and Ogier the Dane and all the rest of the great ones.

When all the peers and lords were assembled before him, King Charlemagne spoke out that thought which was his constant fear, namely:

"Full sorry and bereft is this kingdom, for its fairest and greatest knights lie ravens' meat in the mountain passes. No longer doth Roland sit among you, or Oliver lift his voice in wise counsel. And I am an old man, worn thin by hard years.

"What will chance with France and with those within her borders when I lay down sword and crown at Death's bidding? This is the question I would now have you answer for me.

"Name you now my successor, for time hangs like a heavy cloak about my shoulders and this crown, which was but a featherweight in the days of my youth, is now a circle of lead wearing grievously upon my white head.

"Aye, I have two sons. But neither one can I with a clear conscience bring before you and say, 'This is he who shall sit on the throne in my room.'

"For the younger, Louis, is still but a stripling in years, untried and unproven, and so no king for a troubled age. As for the elder, Charlot—a bringer of sorrow has he already been in times past. Did he not give freedom to his red temper and strike down the son of Ogier, thus near calling ruin upon us all? Therefore, if you think it well to set aside Charlot, although I do love him well, I shall not say you nay. For a kingdom is like unto a new-broke stallion, a firm and knowing hand must hold the guiding rein.

"Now among yourselves do you ponder this matter and your words shall be my will."

Having so spoken the King withdrew into an inner chamber and the peers glanced uneasily at one another, no man wishing to speak before his neighbor lest his words be thought foolish and of small merit.

But Duke Naymes, having reason to fear no man there, arose then and spoke, all listening to him.

"Since our Lord King hath laid this task upon us let us acquit ourselves as becomes peers of France. The King hath spoken truly concerning Prince Louis. He is but a youth who hath never been put to the test, nor has he yet known the weight of mail, or held a full course against the enemy in the open field. Therefore he is no proper leader for knights in war, nor does he yet have the full wisdom of a man.

"But Prince Charlot is of greater years and hath held his place in battle. True, he hath done much that was foolish and devil, but how does a man learn wisdom, save through the sharpness of his own wrongdoing? And perhaps the

Prince hath long since learned the errors of his hot-tempered youth and now governs himself as befits a knight of honor. Also, he is of the true blood of kings and if we now set him aside there will be no peace in the land when King Charlemagne is dead. For there will be those who will follow Charlot to the death and we shall have brother against brother and father aginst son in unnatural war. It will end in the ruin of us all.

"Therefore I now say and urge upon you all, my lords, choose Charlot to come after the king so that our future may be one of peace."

The peers and lords were well pleased at this advice, for the truth of the Duke's words was plain, even to the slowest of wit among them. So they sent one of their number to wait upon the King with the knowledge that they had made their choice. And he straightway returned to the council chamber.

Duke Naymes then spake aloud the will of the peers—namely, that Prince Charlot be king after his father. And King Charlemagne was well pleased and more merry than he had been for many a long day. For greatly did he love his son and he was proud that the peers would choose Charlot who, for his sins in the past, was much hated in the land.

Now among the lords in council was one, Earl Amaury, who was of the same black traitor blood as that twice-damned villain Gannelon (he who betrayed Roland and his fellow knights to their deaths). And this Amaury was as foul a rogue as Gannelon himself. But he was also fair of face and pleasant of voice, very courteous to those who could serve him in some wise. So was the depth of his evil soul hidden to most men and Charlemagne had made him governor to Prince Charlot.

Only one of the great lords had ever suspected that it was Amaury who had taught the young Prince much of the wickedness which he practiced. And that lord was Duke Sevin who ruled wisely and well the rich duchies of Bordeaux and Aquitaine. Although Sevin was dead these many years, Amaury's hate for him was so great that even death could not still it and, since he could not attack Sevin, he planned revenge against the Duke's two young sons, Huon

8

and Gerard. These youths he swore secretly to bring to ruin and shameful death.

With this deep in his snake-brain, he arose now and, smiling as he ever did, addressed the King, saying:

"Lord King, young men must learn many things in this hard world and he who would rule a kingdom hath doubly much to master. Therefore, while you are yet amongst us to advise and oversee him, let Prince Charlot be given a dukedom to hold, that he may learn to govern the larger in the smaller."

The King nodded at the wit in this, as did the other peers. But Duke Naymes drummed with his nails upon the broad arm of his chair, for he had been friend to Duke Sevin and had heard much from him concerning the foulness of Amaury. So that now he suspected a wrong in the making.

"There is," Amaury, encouraged by the King's smiles, continued, "a fair duchy, rich and mighty, meet for any prince, which is forfeit to Your Majesty because of the rash rebellion of its natural lords. Let this be given now to Prince Charlot for his testing."

King Charlemagne showed open surprise, for he could not remember any rebel duchy. And he asked:

"Name you this Duke who is rebel against us."

Amaury replied readily and openly enough:

"My Lord King, I speak of Bordeaux which is forfeit to Your Grace, since Huon and his brother Gerard who now rule there have not come to your court to do homage for their lands—as is your will and the law of France. Duke Sevin, their father, is long dead, and yet never have their faces been seen among your lords."

Then did Duke Naymes rise up in such haste as to nigh overturn his chair of state. Black with anger was his face and hot his voice as he made answer:

"The truth of this matter is otherwise, Lord King. When Sevin, who was much loved amongst us and for good cause, departed into Paradise, his sons were but green youths, untried in judgment or battle. And in their names the Duchess Aclis hath ruled these many years. Greatly did she love Sevin and greatly does she love these sons of his who are much like him as he was in the days of his first youth. Therefore she cannot bear that they go from her or that they be placed in any risk. So have they not yet come to court by reason of their tender years and their mother's great love for them—and not because of any willful rebellion against Your Grace. In proof of my words—send now to Bordeaux and summon these two!"

As Naymes spoke, King Charlemagne remembered well Duke Sevin and bethought himself that the sons of such a worthy father could not be judged rebels without good cause. So he called to him two trusty knights and laid these commands upon them:

"Go you now to the city of Bordeaux and there seek out the sons of Duke Sevin and his lady, the Duchess Aclis. And in my name bid them come to court that they may do homage and be confirmed in their father's lands according to the laws of France. Mark you well how they make you welcome and whether they pay you the full honors becoming those who carry the King's words. And then return hither at all speed and report how you were received."

And the knights rode with their men for Bordeaux but Earl Amaury's hate grew even hotter against Huon and his brother and he went away to plot in secret for their undoing.

II. HOW HUON RECEIVED THE KING'S COMMAND AND AMAURY PLOTTED HIS RUIN

WHEN THOSE knights who played herald at the order of the King reached the fair and pleasant city of Bordeaux they rode straight to the Keep of that city where lived and held court the Duchess Aclis and her sons. And these same youthful lords had but that hour returned from the chase so that they stood yet in the courtyard, each bearing upon his wrist his gerfalcon, hooded and jessed.

But when the King's men made known their presence Huon did come forward to greet them in great eagerness and with his own hand did he hold the stirrup of the eldest knight for his dismounting, showing him the courtesy which he would have paid to the King himself. Right pleasantly too did the Duchess Aclis and Lord Gerard welcome them, receiving them with all honors, so that the knights were much pleased, saying privately to one another:

"Were our Lord King here these lords of Bordeaux could show him no better greeting than they have given to us."

When they had refreshed themselves from their journey and could want no comfort, then did Huon ask of them their business and why Charlemagne had so sent them to Bordeaux. And the eldest made reply for them all:

"It is the will of our lord and dread master, King Charlemagne of France, that the sons of Duke Sevin come unto him and join his court that they may be made known unto their brother peers and confirmed in their lands as is the law."

The Duchess Aclis hastened to make answer, saying:

"If our Lord King hath now any fault to find with my dear sons because they have not sought his court before, let the full weight of his just anger fall upon me. When my gracious lord, Duke Sevin, departed from me into the realm beyond our stars, he left me desolate and fearful, with but infants to comfort me. In their childish faces I saw ever my lord and I could not bear that they should go out of my keeping, even for the space of an hour. But now that they are men grown—though still of tender years—I can no longer rule their lives by a woman's jealous fears. Let them but wait until after the Easter season so that once more we may celebrate together the Rising of Our Lord Jesu, and I shall surrender them to the King so that they may become his men in all things, even as was their noble father."

Huon arose then, his comely face shining with pride and pleasure, and said to the King's messengers:

"Go then to our Lord King and say unto him that we are much honored by his commands and shall speedily set forth to appear at his court, obeying only this last wish of our lady mother, that we celebrate the Rising of Christ by her side. Take you also, in remembrance of this meeting, these coursers of the Orkney breed—may they bear you faithfully and well into the heart of battle or over the roads of peace—

11

and with them take also the knights' cloaks which hang upon their saddles and the purses looped therewith. For to the messengers of a King no man can do too much honor."

Then were the King's knights indeed amazed, for such costly gifts were the largess of a great lord. And with great joy they did put on the fine silken cloaks of deep crimson and mount the war stallions. Many thanks did they say before they rode again through the gates of Bordeaux.

And when they returned to the King's court they spoke together and severally concerning Huon and his brother and the open-handed Duchess. Too much praise they could not give to the lords and lady of Bordeaux.

"Lord Huon," said the eldest knight, "is even yet but a slender stripling but he is princelike in his courtesy and fine speaking. He is the most comely of face and person, the finest lordling, that I have seen within the borders of France since our beloved Roland was a youth. And his brother Gerard is like unto him, though not as mighty a warrior as yet, being slighter of person and younger of years. Greatly do the twain of them honor Your Grace and much eagerness to come to you do they show, staying only with their mother until after the Eastertide that they may obey her last request."

His messengers then showed the King the princely gifts which had been made them and he was astonished and greatly pleased to see such honor shown to his knights. So he did vow before the assembled lords and peers:

"In the days which are now long past Duke Sevin of Bordeaux was cup-brother and sword-mate to us and he was loved even as a brother of our own blood. Worthy was he of all good will and high honor and now it seems that he hath left behind him on this earth two sons bred of his spirit as well as of his flesh. For as this young Lord Huon hath treated my messengers, so did his father render homage in the old days to those to whom honor was due.

"Such young lords will be ornaments to our assemblage. And I do swear that when they come hither Huon shall be proclaimed a peer of France, even as he will be confirmed in his holding of Bordeaux and Aquitaine. And Gerard shall

12

be made a member of our own household to his advancement."

All the lords and peers agreed with the King's words—save Amaury, who, seeing such a sorry end to his hopes of ruin for Sevin's sons, knew that he must plot anew. And in his dark mind an evil plan began to grow.

He hurried from the council hall of the King into the apartments of Prince Charlot where he found the King's son dallying at ease with some young knights and squires of his following. And there Amaury did fling himself on his knees before the Prince, to clutch at Charlot's cloak and cry aloud for justice.

The Prince, much amazed at Amaury's outcry, did send the others from him and demand that the Earl tell him the cause of such distracted actions. Then did Amaury display the blackness of his heart in the words of his crooked mouth.

"Know you, Prince Charlot, your father, deceived by false enemies, is bringing hither to court that traitor Huon of Bordeaux and his brother Gerard. And our King promises to bestow upon Huon the duchies of Bordeaux and Aquitaine which should be rightfully yours. While Gerard the King promises to take into his household where he may secretly work all manner of ill. Once here at court they will work against Your Grace, for this Huon and his brother come of bad stock and me they hate so that they will even seek to injure you—since you have played my friend—bringing ruin upon the man through his master. So do I warn you now, Prince Charlot, if these twain enter into this court black evil will come with them and none—even the highest—shall be safe from their wickedness."

Now was Charlot alarmed at the words of Amaury for in his heart he knew well that he was not well beloved in France and that many of the lords hated him for his ill deeds of the past. So, should Huon and Gerard come to work against him secretly, they would find many to listen to them. Thus, with all his fears and hate aroused, Charlot prayed Amaury to tell him what to do to defend himself against these brothers from Bordeaux.

And Amaury advised Charlot to arm and horse divers of

his men and meet secretly with him, Amaury, without the city that they might arrange to deal with Huon and Gerard before they reached the King's court. Eagerly enough Charlot agreed.

III. HOW AMAURY AND CHARLOT DID LIE IN AMBUSH AND WHAT CHANCED THEREFROM

THE FEAST OF Easter being over Huon and Gerard did prepare to keep their promise to the King. Choosing from among their men divers knights and squires, they did clothe them anew from helm to spur with cunningly made armor that they might make a goodly sight at court. But Huon and Gerard donned no mail, nor did the younger brother even buckle sword belt about him. For they were minded to journey in peace and safety under the protection of the King.

Huon, however, did put on him that sword belt wrought of fine silver and gold which Duke Sevin had worn in war and peace, and from it did hang that good blade, forged far across the seas in the unknown Easter lands by Demons of the Night (or so said the simple folk of the country) which Sevin had swung in battle ofttimes before—to King Charlemagne's great gain. But of body armor Huon had none, only went at ease in tunic and cloak.

Duchess Aclis wept full sore to see her sons depart thus from Bordeaux. For never since their hour of birth had the twain not been where her eye might sight upon them and now her heart misgave her strangely, for she had secretly dwelt upon all those evils which might chance while Huon and Gerard were apart from her. But of this she said naught lest she shadow the brightness of their adventure and she hid her many tears behind her veil.

Gerard did not ride so boldly forth from the gate, nor did he spur his horse into the freshness of the morning beyond the city. Rather did he amble soberly at the pace of one who goes unwillingly upon a disliked errand so that Huon must needs rein back to company him. And when his brother laughingly chid him for his snail-like creeping, Gerard surprised Huon beyond measure with a breathless answer:

"Brother, I fear me that no good will come to either of us from this venture. Let us back to Bordeaux and that speedily!"

Loud indeed then did Huon laugh, and cry that his brother was a babe and already crying for his mother's arms. But Gerard showed no anger at this taunt. Rather he turned once more and gazed with great longing at the towers and walls of Bordeaux.

"Evil lies before us," he continued. "Aye, great evil comes of this journey. Last night I did dream that I rode on this same highway and out of the bushes there did spring upon us a raging leopard, his jaws agape with hunger. Me he did bear to earth and rend with dripping fangs so that my soul was driven from my body and I was dead. But you, my brother, escaped his fury. So plain was my dream that I do deem it a warning sent from Heaven that we should not travel on this way—"

But Huon shook his head. "More likely it be an omen sent by the Devil to tempt us from our duty to the King, so that we will break our pledged word. See—this day is fair and the countryside most good to look upon. Our road is smooth before us and behind ride twenty good knights and squires to serve us well. Put aside your foolish fears, Gerard, they are but shadows and no fit musing for a grown knight."

So Gerard spoke no more. But in his heart he knew anger against his brother, that Huon would so easily dismiss his warning. And he thought that long had it been thus, that Huon, bold and fearless and taking little heed for the future, had set aside the cautions of his younger brother. Yet Huon was loved and praised by all and he, Gerard, was deemed a youngling, not to be given serious heed.

Before nightfall they met with the worthy Abbot of Cluny who was also on his way to court. And both the brothers were most glad to see him, for he was their well-beloved uncle. So did they join their party to his and that night all lay together in friendship at an abbey he chose to visit.

Again in the morning, after breaking their fast, they rode

on together and all went very well with them until they
reached the top of a hill and could see where the road
wound down into the leafy lip of a wood. Huon pulled back
his mount and those with him, wondering at his act, did
likewise.

Then he pointed out to the company certain flashes of light
among the trees below—as if men clad in mail moved there.
And so the party hesitated, not knowing what lay before
them, hidden in that wood.

Since they were not men of war, the Abbot and his monks
and laymen withdrew to the side of the road, and the
churchman spoke frankly to Huon, saying:

"Fair sir, I and all my followers are men of peace and
good will. If evil men lie in ambush before us, surely they
must mean ill to you who ride with armor on your backs
and swords at your sides. Therefore, since of war I can have
no part, we needs must separate here and go our several ways.
For if I shed blood, even in the defending of my own, I
have committed black sin. But you are a man of strife and
bred to conflict."

And, as the Abbot was speaking so, out of the trees below
a Knight, masked by the lowered visor of his helmet, spurred
his horse so that he now barred the path of all who would
come down the hill. There he sat silently waiting.

After looking upon this barrier of knight and horse most
closely, Huon said to his brother:

"There is no reason for either of us to fear aught of any
man living, for we have no quarrels hanging above our heads.
You wear no armor, nor do you bear a sword, so all can see
that you ride in peace with the world. Get you down
now into the valley and ask of that knight what he would
have of us."

And Gerard obeyed his brother. Coming down into the
valley of the wood he reined in his mount before the silent
knight and addressed him boldly.

"Good sir, what do you wish of us who would quarrel
with no man this day? Know you, I am Gerard of Bordeaux
and yonder is my brother Huon, Duke of that same city. We
are bound, by the King's own command, to the court of

Charlemagne. Therefore stay us not, lest the justice of the King demand an accounting from you—"

Now the masked knight was Prince Charlot, the King's son. But he was not minded to speak to Gerard his rightful name. Instead he answered the boy despitefully and with much anger, saying:

"Rash youth, know you that I am son to Duke Thierry, he who hath many times been injured by those of your house. And now I am here to end all his wrongs upon your bodies—doing to death you and that proud cockerel who sits yonder daring to name himself Duke of Bordeaux. The lands of Bordeaux are by all rights mine!"

Gerard being warned by the anger of the knight's speech would have then fled. But his mount stumbled and Charlot bore down upon the helpless youth, his lance in crouch. Deep into Gerard's tender flesh struck the steel so that he was borne from his horse and fell heavily upon the packed earth of the road, and from his side there poured a thick flood of rich blood so that he swooned. Thus he did not hear Charlot's loud shout of:

"So do I serve mine enemies. As you lie, so shall fall that other dog of Bordeaux!"

But Huon heard that shout and his heart was white-hot with his rage for he believed his young brother dead—foully slain without defense by this masked murderer. And his temper broke all bonds so that to him the whole world was as red as the blood still flowing from Gerard's slight body.

IV. HOW HUON DID SLAY THE KING'S SON AND RODE TO COURT FOR JUSTICE

WHEN HUON SAW his loved brother Gerard lying as one dead in a spreading pool of his own blood, his rage did so rise within him that he took no heed of those about him or of aught else in the whole world save that villain who had struck down the unarmed boy. Drawing that good sword

which had so long served his father, Duke Sevin, Huon rode down the hill to meet the unknown knight.

And Charlot, seeing his enemy coming so wildly and recklessly upon him, unarmed save for a sword, with no mail upon his body or helm upon his head, looked forward to an easy battle. He set ready his lance and urged his mount forward to the kill.

But Huon was no untried swordster and, seeing how this stranger meant to spit him cleanly upon lance point, he gathered his cloak about his arm and flung it at the lance—at the same time throwing his body to one side. Thus did Charlot's lance become entangled in the folds of cloth and Huon passed unharmed by the charge although the sharp point of steel pierced his tunic and bruised the flesh beneath.

As Charlot strove to throw away his lance and free his sword from its scabbard, Huon struck. And so sharp and heavy was the blow that the Prince fell from his charger and was dead even before his body rolled in the roadway.

Huon troubled not to lift the visor of his dead enemy or look closely upon him whom he had killed. Rather did he busy himself with searching out the deep wound in Gerard's side and binding the yet-welling slash with linen torn from his own back. Having so rudely stanched his brother's hurt he lifted him up, still a-swoon, into the saddle of his horse and walked beside him out of the valley, leaving the dead Prince in the road alone.

Speedily was Huon joined by the knights and men of his following. And they urged that all must travel without pause lest the companions of the dead knight come out of the wood to cut them down. And all armed themselves for such an attack.

But when they reached again the party of the Abbot of Cluny, he bade them take heart for he had seen, from the hilltop, men come out of the wood to bear away the stranger. And none of these had set out on Huon's trail.

Huon's anger was still hot and his heart was dark with misgiving as he looked upon the white face and drooping body of his brother. And out of his deep foreboding he spoke to his men:

19

"Cursed be King Charlemagne if this deed was of his planning! If it was his secret purpose to so put an end to the line of Sevin—then has he lost. For while I live and stand upright on my two feet and have an arm strong enough to swing my father's sword, I shall avenge this foul deed. Even in the very beard of the King shall I speak my mind concerning this. For such treachery there is no pardon—that we should be so enticed to our deaths!"

And naught that the Abbot could say would abate the great rage of Huon which was ever freshly kindled by the sight of Gerard who now and again moaned and cried aloud upon the name of Our Lord Jesu for reason of the keen pain of his hurt.

Meanwhile the Earl Amaury did issue forth from his ambush in the wood to speak sharply to those about the body of Charlot, ordering them to take up the dead Prince and tie him across his own saddle. Then, leading the burdened charger with his own hand he, too, rode to the King's court, followed by his men and those of Charlot's household. On the way he thought much of the ill he could now do to Huon because of this slaying and how he might best arouse the King's full wrath against the youth from Bordeaux.

First to reach the court of Charlemagne was Huon and his party. And straight into the King's presence they strode, bearing with them on a litter, fashioned of cloaks and lances, the swooning Gerard.

All those assembled there—peers, nobles and King—were much astounded at such a coming but Huon went boldly to the foot of the throne and cried aloud so that all fell silent to hear him:

"Is this the justice of King Charlemagne?"

The pride of his bearing was such that anger arose in the King's throat for no man had so fronted him since the days of his youth. And he would have made swift return to such insolence but he was minded to know the wherefore of this strange entrance. So he made reply in more moderate voice than those of his following expected to hear, saying:

"How now, stripling. Why comest thou hither in such

clamor demanding to know of our justice? Who are you and who is this youth you bear on a litter?"

"Know you, Lord King," returned Huon, still proud of bearing, "I am that Huon of Bordeaux, son to Duke Sevin, whom you by royal decree did summon to you. And this be my brother Gerard who lies here sore stricken because, though wearing no sword or armor, he was set upon most foully by a full armored knight.

"Was it by your pleasure that we were so waylaid and attacked? If it was—look you now upon your handiwork and rejoice, noble King!"

Quickly Huon stooped and tore away the cloak which was wrapped about Gerard so that all might see the stained linen about his wound and how the rising blood made it like unto a corselet of ruby.

Then did Huon draw his sword and set it before him. And the torches and cresslights picked out the shining steel save where the blood of Charlot, now dried, dimmed the gleam.

"Look you here also, Lord King. These stains are the blood of the murderer who now lies dead himself—and by my hand. For so do we of Bordeaux pay just debts!"

King Charlemagne looked upon Gerard even as Huon had bade him and his heart was moved to see so fair a youth lying in such extremity. No longer was his anger turned against Huon, but rather against those who had wrought so ill a deed. And when he made answer it was a firm promise.

"Hotly do you speak, Lord Huon. But if I stood so, doubtless my words would also be aheat with just anger. Know you that this deed is as foul in my eyes as it is in yours and he who did it shall be searched out—if he who planned it was not the same who struck down your brother and was so fitly punished! Listen, all ye assembled here, it was by my will that these youths were summoned hither and what touches them, touches also me. Therefore they shall be as my sons and do you so receive them.

"Bring hither those skilled in leechcraft and let them look to the wounds of the Lord Gerard that he may be comforted."

So was it done as the King commanded and the leeches did say that Gerard would be healed of his hurt.

But for Charlot there was no healing in this world and Amaury thought only of how to turn the Prince's death to his own account.

V. OF THE EVIL AMAURY WROUGHT WITH HIS LYING TONGUE

Now AT SUNSET of that same day there came riding into the King's city the Earl Amaury leading Charlot's charger with its master's body bound upon its back. And as he rode within the gates Amaury raised a great wailing cry of grief, as did all those who rode with him. So hearing this sad lament the townspeople gathered and they too wept at such a woeful sight. Straight into the presence of Charlemagne did Amaury ride, finding the King at wine with Huon and the other peers.

Before the King, Amaury did unloose the body of the Prince so that it slipped to the floor with a crash of armor and lay at the father's feet. Then the traitor Earl cried aloud so that all there did hark unto him, saying:

"Look you upon the body of Prince Charlot who has been most foully done to death. Slain, my King and lords, by this villain who dares to sit now in the high seat of honor—namely, Huon of Bordeaux!"

Huon, looking closely at the body, knew it for that of the knight who had wounded Gerard and later fallen by his own sword. And he marveled at Amaury's words for he had not knowingly struck down Charlot. So that now he made answer quietly enough:

"Lord King, this corpse lying here is that of the stranger knight who did wound my brother and whom I did kill in fit punishment for so black a deed—my brother being unarmed—"

But while he yet spoke Amaury dropped to his knees and

freed the head of the dead man from its helmet so that all
there assembled might see the still face. And from the throat
of the old King there broke a pitiful cry. Deeply had he
loved Charlot and here now lay his son, slain in the full pride
of his youth.

"My son!" That cry rang through the hall and pierced the
hearts of all who heard it, for the depth of the King's sorrow
was bared in his words.

"Aye, your son, Lord King. And there stands the false
Huon whom you cherish and yet who hath killed Charlot.
We were hunting in the forest as the Prince was wont to do
and, having loosed his falcon against fair prey, he was vexed
when the bird returned not—so he needs must pursue it.
Whilst we rode so, unheeding of our path, we came upon a
road where this suckling rogue was passing, the Prince's
own falcon upon his wrist. When Prince Charlot demanded
that his own be returned to him this same Huon and his
brother set upon the Prince, cutting him down without
mercy!"

When he heard such lies the rage arose within Huon so
that at first it choked speech from him. But he cast his glove
so that it struck the Earl full across his false lips.

"Thou liest!" cried the young lord of Bordeaux when he
could again command his voice.

But King Charlemagne had made a secret sign to his
guards to take the Duke, and that they now did, bearing
him down with their strength and binding fast his arms in
spite of his struggles.

"Strike off the head of this murderer!" roared the King.

But, as his guards would have obeyed, Duke Naymes
held him off, saying:

"By all the laws of chivalry and knighthood, we cannot
so use this youth. He hath named Amaury 'Liar' and hath
challenged him to prove the truth of his tale with his body—
Our Lord God standing as the Judge of both. Such is his
right and no earthly King may take it from him!"

Charlemagne was dour with wrath but he saw that all
the peers and lords of the court were of Naymes' mind and,
that if he wrought his will upon Huon, trouble would come

of it. So he was forced to agree. But he did so grudgingly and with black hatred in his heart.

"Let them fight according to the uses of chivalry," he said slowly. "And may God bring justice to this murderer. But likewise may it be recorded now that if either be slain before he confesses fault in the matter, then the other is straightway banished from this realm never to return!"

A strong outcry arose from all because of this injustice—for all knew that either might be killed in the heat of battle in such a way that he would have no time for confession. Naymes spoke strongly to the King, but to no avail, and Charlemagne's will in this was so set that no man might sway him.

Huon then went forth with Naymes who was pledged to keep him safe against the morrow when he would meet Amaury in the field. And the Earl withdrew likewise leaving court and King to mourn the fallen Prince.

VI. HOW HUON DEALT WITH AMAURY IN COMBAT AND THE DOOM LAID UPON HIM THEREAFTER

EARLY IN THE morning his squires came in to Huon where he lay in the hold of Duke Naymes and roused him from his sleep. On his body they did put fair clean linen and over that a hauberk of leather. Then did the Duke bring to the youth fine mail wrought by craftsmen working to his own secret pattern. This Huon discovered to be light yet supple so that he who wore it was as one free from armor. So armed he rode for the field yet fasting, a war stallion of the color of fresh spilled blood between his knees, Duke Naymes on his right hand and the squire of his body going before with his plumed helmet and shield.

Since Huon rode thus uncovered all those about the field marveled at his youth and the comeliness of his features, saying amongst themselves that not even a king's son in his pride could equal this Duke out of Bordeaux. Such whisperings reached even to the ears of Charlemagne where he sat in state and they fanned the hotter his wrath against the slayer of his son.

Amaury came to the place of combat with an easy mind, for he deemed Huon but a green boy with no knowledge of lance or sword play, no fit match for a warrior of many years' seasoning. But, as he rode into the view of the court, his black charger stumbled so that the Earl, who was riding easy, was near to being unhorsed. And those watching felt this to be a dark omen.

But Amaury straightened in his saddle and put on his helmet with a steady hand, having confidence in himself and his strength.

Huon too put on his helmet, slung his shield upon his arm and took up the lance his squire held ready. His bright roan pawed the turf and thundered a challenge of its own to the black which Amaury curbed with a heavy hand.

Then, at the word given by the King himself, they charged. Amaury aimed his lance at Huon's helmet. He knew such a stroke to be a master one which only a skillful man might dare to attempt—yet so sure was he of the coming battle that he might have been a boy teasing a harmless kitten.

But Huon chose the safer attack, guessing at what might lie in Amaury's mind. So that when they met in their course he swung aside his head and the Earl's lance thrust only into the thinness of air. But Huon's lance struck straight and true into the center of the other's shield with such force that not only Amaury but also his attacker were hurled from their saddles.

On foot both cast aside their useless lances and drew their swords. And the Earl was so angered by his overthrow that without caution he came against Huon, having even thrown from him his shield that he might strike a two-handed blow.

Huon still clung to his shield and with it he caught the blow which Amaury aimed to cut him down. Deep into the iron stove the blade in such a way that the Earl could not speedily withdraw it again. Then did Huon strike in his turn, so clean a blow where neck met shoulder that the strong mail Amaury was wearing was but as a piece of silk. And Amaury's head, still within his plumed helm, rolled across the dusty ground, even to the very foot of the King's chair.

Those gathered about the lists raised a cry of amazement, for no one of them had really believed in his heart that Huon could overcome Amaury. And the King's crafty heart leaped also—for if Huon were not dead in truth, he would speedily be dead to France—since Amaury had been killed before confessing falseness. And so did the heralds proclaim the King's will at his signal.

When the harsh decree of banishment was read, all the lords about the throne raised their voices in protest and Duke Naymes led their outcry, saying:

"Lord King, what sorrow will you do with these hard words? This youth hath proved in battle, with God judging the right, that he spoke true words before you. Since he slew Prince Charlot unwittingly, he is not to be thought a murderer. Do you devise some punishment which will not set him for all his lifetime far from those who hold him dear!"

King Charlemagne's anger was waxing strong, but also did he see that his lords were in open rebellion against him in this matter. So he spoke quietly, as if he had been moved by the speech of Naymes.

"Truly Huon hath done much evil—taking from me in my old age the son of my heart and from France her king to be. But likewise is it true that God Himself hath given this youth victory in this strife. Therefore, lest I be too harsh I shall lay upon Huon a quest, such as was the custom of chivalry in bygone times. And he is not to return to France— under the pain of shameful death—until this quest be successfully finished. What say you to that, Duke Naymes?"

Naymes, seeing that the King could be moved no farther in Huon's behalf, assented with a bowed head.

"This then is the quest of Huon of Bordeaux," proclaimed Charlemagne. "Let him go out of France into the very stronghold of the Saracens—the City of Babylon. There he must go into the court of Emir Gaudys who ruleth that city. And he shall take from the chin of Gaudys a handful of the beard which groweth there, from the mouth of Gaudys shall he take five teeth, and from the body of Gaudys' chief lord shall he strike the head—cutting it off in the full sight of all who are men of Gaudys. To me he shall bring this hair and teeth. In addition he must salute upon the mouth Gaudys' daughter—in sight of her father's court!"

Now when Huon heard the conditions of the quest his heart was desolate for he believed that no living man, unless he had more than mortal assistance, could survive such deeds. And so he said to King and court:

"My King, you send now to his certain death one who has wished you well all his days. May all men hearing my story in times hereafter judge between us."

Then he said no more but went to the bedside of his brother Gerard into whose keeping he gave Bordeaux and his other lands. Then, taking a sorrowful farewell of Gerard, he chose divers knights and squires of his following and set forth to obey the commands of the King.

VII. HOW HUON DEPARTED FROM FRANCE AND GERARD RULED IN BORDEAUX

WITH A HEART full of sorrow Huon took ship with his men and sailed to the ancient land of Italy where they came at length to that city which lies in the center of the world, namely, Rome. And there did the young Duke beg audience with the Holy Father. And His Holiness was pleased to receive him, saying:

"Long ago was thy father close to me and now it giveth me happiness to look upon the son of his body who is truly made after the same good fashion as my ancient friend—for of thee, Huon of Bordeaux, I have heard only good report. Tell me now, my son, what has brought thee from France to our gates?"

Then did Huon give tongue to all the evil which had fastened upon him and tell of the hard task laid upon him by Charlemagne. And he spoke full sadly of his future, saying that he knew that he now rode to his death. But when such words crossed his lips, His Holiness stopped him with upraised hand and chid him gently thus:

"My son, know you that all things are possible to him who believeth upon Our Gracious Lord—even as He Himself hath said. Go you forth armed in faith and you shall conquer—yea, even though against you stand in mailed might all the awful forces of the heathen."

And at these words Huon's heart was lightened of a heavy care and he was as a man who has been freed from heavy chains. His Holiness then bid Huon seek out the Duke Garyn, he who was kin to Duke Sevin and now abode at St. Omar. And Huon did as he was commanded, finding Garyn a knight of no little renown, well marked by all the realm of Christendom.

Duke Garyn welcomed the youth with open arms, taking him to his bosom and proclaiming him one to sit in the place of the son and heir he had never known. Because, as he told Huon, the boy was as the Duke Sevin had been in his first youth and Duke Sevin was his own brother. Thus did Huon meet with his uncle and receive much honor and kindness from him.

When the time came that Huon and his men must take ship for the land of the Saracens, Duke Garyn called to him his lady wife and said:

"Look you well, my lady, to the affairs of this duchy for I am minded to sail with my nephew so that he ventures not alone into this great danger."

His lady wept full sore as she replied to her lord thus:

"My good lord, much do I fear to see you go from me, for evil have been my dreams of late and I think that if you go we shall not look upon your face again in this world. But if this be your will then I will say naught. All shall be ordered as you wish and I shall hold your duchy against your return."

Having so spoken she went privately to Huon and asked of him that he would watch over her lord and see that no harm came to him, for deeply did she love the Duke Garyn. And Huon swore upon the Cross that all would be as she asked and no harm would come to his uncle if he, Huon of Bordeaux, could prevent.

But still she wept, hiding her tear-besmeared face in the long sleeves of her robe as Garyn and Huon rode forth from the hold of St. Omar.

Now while Huon journeyed thus half the world away, his brother Gerard, having recovered of the wound dealt him by Prince Charlot, arose from his bed and rode home to Bordeaux. The Duchess Aclis had a man at watch in the tower and when he sighted the pennons on the lances of those in Gerard's company, he called that joyful news to all the keep, bringing the household out in haste to welcome their returning lords.

But when Gerard came alone into the courtyard the Duchess put her hands to her breast as if to ward off a fatal sword thrust and cried:

"Where is thy brother? Why ride you alone?"

So Gerard needs must tell her the whole sorry tale at once. And upon the hearing of it she uttered a shriek, in so loud a voice that all the city heard it and the people trembled at its meaning. So having given voice to her woe she fell as one dead upon the pavement.

Her maidens bore her speedily to her chamber, but she never spoke again, for her heart was broken and she was with her lord in Paradise.

For long dark days Gerard did mourn both mother and brother—for he deemed Huon to be dead also, since no mortal man might safely fulfill the quest Charlemagne had laid upon him. Gerard spoke not to those about him, nor did he break his fast, until at last one of the old knights who had served as his tutor in arms came to him and said:

"My lord, grievous indeed have been these misfortunes laid upon you. But weeping rouses not the dead to life again. Bordeaux needs a lord and you must now take the high seat and rule here, even as did your worthy father and brother before you."

So did Gerard become Duke of Bordeaux and he liked it full well, in time forgetting Huon and the fact that he was only lord in Bordeaux by reason of his brother's ill fortune.

For to him Huon was now as dead as if his body lay in the
tomb of the Dukes. In the past he had known envy of his
brother and had dreamed secret dreams of being great when
Huon was naught. Now he lived those dreams in truth.

After some time he took to wife a daughter of Gyblerde of
Cecyll who was distantly of the blood of that Amaury who
had brought such misfortune to the House of Duke Sevin.
She was a lady of wondrous dark beauty, both witty and
sharp of tongue, and deeply learned in certain black arts
which made her feared by the commoners throughout the
countryside. But of her family Gerard did not think, being
pleased by her person and beguiled by the forbidden
knowledge she held. And he came to listen overmuch to her
words and those of her father, who was as crafty and
double-tongued as any rogue within the borders of France.

And thus did evil enter into Bordeaux without the knowledge of its rightful lord, Duke Huon.

VIII. HOW HUON MET WITH THE HERMIT
GERAMES AND TOOK THE ROAD THROUGH
THE FAIRY WOOD

THE MERCHANT SHIP wherein Huon and the Duke Garyn and
all their train traveled set them ashore upon a barren, cliff-
bound land far from all the cities of the Saracens, for Huon
wished none to know of his coming until he won to Babylon
itself. Taking to horse once more, he and his uncle and
their men rode inland towards the rising sun which was the
way to Babylon.

At length they came upon the edge of a vast wasteland
across which lay open to them two faintly marked paths.
One ran through the waste where could be seen only bare
rock and sand burnt and baked by the fierce sun, with no
trees or other green things to relieve the eye. But the other
way went on into a pleasant woodland where the trees were
a living promise of springs of water.

This road did Huon choose and had turned his charger into it when out of a misshapen hut piled loosely from the desert rocks there sprang one in the rags of a hermit to bar their way.

About his loins was the torn skin of a lion and his gray hair hung in wild ragged locks upon his bone-thin shoulders. A long beard covered him to his girdle, but his eyes were still afire with reason and strength, and he bore himself as one who had once had authority in the world beyond this starved land.

"Pray you, fair sir," he cried unto Huon, "by your dress and the cross you bear upon your shield you are a Christian knight. If you be truly so, heed now the warning of one who, though now fallen on evil times, once held his lands of a Christian king!"

Much astounded by such a greeting, Huon reined in his mount and bade the man speak on, telling how he came to live in so desolate a spot.

"Once was I the Knight Gerames who did ride upon the right hand of good Duke Sevin of Bordeaux. But desiring to look upon the Sepulcher of Our Lord Jesu, I sailed hither and my pilgrim ship was set upon by those wolves of the sea, the pirates of the Crescent. By them, I and all those with me were sold into slavery and after some years I escaped my chains to flee here into the wilderness where none thought to seek me. For in seven years you have been the first to ride these ancient roads. Know you not that these be evil lands for Christian men? What hard fate brought you hither?"

Huon replied with the tale of the quest set upon him and how he and his uncle were on their way now into Babylon to obey the orders of Charlemagne.

When Gerames learned that Huon was son to his old lord, Duke Sevin, tears came out upon his hairy cheeks and he seized upon the youth's hand to kiss it—vowing that he would follow Huon even to the death from that hour forward.

But again he begged them to turn aside from the path through the wood, saying:

"This wood is wrought of magic, being one of those strange places where the world of Fairy touches upon the world of men. Oberon who is king among the People of the Hills is wont to ride among those trees with his Fairy lords. And should he sight a mortal man and speak to him, and that man replyeth—why then the mortal is under the spell of Fairy and must do all which Oberon requireth of him for all his days. Many powerful and sturdy knights have been so lost."

Huon looked again at the burning heat of the desert land and saw how there was lacking there all manner of shade and other refreshment. And then he turned to the cool promised by the woodland and it drew him strangely. He asked:

"How does it chance if the mortal answers not the words of King Oberon? Is he still caught up in the Fairy spell?"

Gerames shook his head. "Nay. Unless a man speaketh to King Oberon, the Lord of Fairies holdeth no power over him."

"Then," said Huon, "shall we keep our tongues within our jaws and be safe even if the dread king meets us. Beneath this hot sun we shall surely fail and die if we go into the desert, but if we go by the forest way we shall have shade and water to sustain us."

So did they ride by the wood road even though Gerames still prophesied that ill would come of it. When they came into the heart of the forest they heard the sound of a huntsman's silver horn and into sight galloped a fair company of knights clad all in that green which is the favorite color of those from the Hills.

He who kept to the fore was a youth of such shining beauty that his like has never been seen in the world of mortal men. And splendid was his dress, the green being overlaid with much silver and gold, and his sword belt set with rows of gleaming pearls, his knight's spurs roweled with diamonds.

But in stature he was but a small child and on his black horse he appeared as a boy of ten years until you saw the wisdom and maturity of his face.

Seeing Huon and his company the small youth did halt

his chase and he put down on his saddlebow the horn he had been sounding to say:

"How now, proud mortal. Who are you who dares to come within the boundaries of my kingdom?" And to all their ears his voice had the sweetness of open song.

But Huon and those with him remembered the warning of Gerames and they made no answer, so that King Oberon was angered by their discourtesy.

"Sit clapp-fast, ye villains!" he cried. "And see what your clownishness will cost you!"

He then put spur to his mount and rode off, his lords behind him. While Gerames said to Huon:

"Lord, let us make haste out of this wood for I think that this Fairy King means us some mischief."

Thus did Huon and all his company use whip and spur and tried to speed out of that ill-omened wood. But before they reached its outer fringe there arose such a tempest as no man of that party had seen before.

Trees were torn by the wind to fall across their way and there came down upon them much water as if a river had been gathered up from its bed to be thrown at these invading mortals. Grievous was their plight and Huon feared that here he would end his quest, nevermore to see the high towers of Bordeaux.

IX. HOW HUON MADE HIS PEACE WITH OBERON AND GAINED THEREBY

As THE TEMPEST encompassed them about and the spears of the wind thrust in upon them, those who were with Huon cried out against their sore fate and bewailed this death which was now coming to them in a land so far from all they loved. Some of them spoke out against Huon, saying that he had brought them to this ill pass and that the storm had risen from the wrath of King Oberon, for no wind not born of magic could be so fierce. This did Huon likewise believe and answered his men thus:

"Aye, by my lack of thought has this evil come to us—so that the innocent suffer beside me for my folly. Would that I might behold once more the dread King of Fairy and plead with him for the lives of you who have faithfully followed me even to this pass—"

And, even as he so spoke into the jaws of that horrific wind, they heard, above the screech of the storm, the silver notes of a hunting horn. Across the fallen trees cantered the small lord of that forbidden world, still followed by his Elf knights. Close did he ride to where those of the mortal world huddled and he addressed Huon, saying:

"Who art thou who comes riding hither without leave of any of our world?"

And Huon, although Gerames plucked warningly at his sleeve, made quick answer.

"My Lord King, I am Huon, sometime Duke of Bordeaux within the real of France, now riding exiled as a simple knight upon a quest set me by King Charlemagne because of his hot anger against me."

"And what crime didst thou commit to set so generous a king, known alike to our world and yours, against you?" queried Oberon.

"No crime save to defend myself against death," declared Huon boldly. And he took heart, for about them now the tempest was stayed, no waters came nigh and the wind had died away. So did he make known to Oberon all that had befallen him since that long-ago day when he had left the gates of Bordeaux to attend the court of France.

"Ill indeed has been your fortune," observed the Fairy King. "No mortal can do what the King has demanded of you and come alive through the doing of it. But what a mortal cannot do, those of my realm can. Therefore, since you have been the first man in full five hundred years to speak me boldly, I shall give to you certain aids—which, if you use them wisely, may win you what you desire.

"First—see you this horn? At my birth certain spells were set upon it by the wise women from beyond the end of the world. Gloriande did enchant it so that a soft note from it does blast all illness known to man or fairy. Two notes bring end to all hunger and thirst—by the decree of the Lady Translyne. Blow yet louder upon it, said the Lady Margole, and the heavy heart shall be lightened and all sorrow fade from the mind. While a strong blast has the power to summon aid to your side in time of trouble, by the will of the Wise Lempatrix. This horn will I give unto you, asking only that you use it with full wisdom, not idly as might a child in play. For when you sound the note set by Lempatrix I, myself, and all my company must obey its summons to fight beside you."

Oberon then took from about his neck the chain which held this wondrous horn and dropped it about Huon's shoulders so that it lay upon the young knight's breast, and he stood dumbstruck at such a gift. The Fairy King waited not for any thanks but drew from the folds of his tunic a cup of pearl and silver which, in that dark forest, shone with a rosy light of its own.

"This too is a treasure, equal in worth to the horn of many voices, for he who carries it need never thirst, also will he be warned as to what manner of company he keeps. If an honest man raises this cup to his lips he shall find it full of the finest wine. But should one of a dark and evil heart seek to drink, the cup shall be as the desert sand, empty and sere. Take thou this, also, that it may serve you in its own way."

The cup was put into Huon's two hands and he stood staring into it. After a long moment he dared to raise it to his lips and it was as Oberon had promised, brimming rich and rare with wine. Deep did the young knight drink and yet when he held the cup from him it was stil brim deep. So did Huon then pass it to Garyn and so about the company and for all of them it remained full. And from their drinking all were greatly heartened and knew no more thirst.

Many were the thanks which Huon did give to Oberon for the gift of these so great treasures but the only reply the Fairy King would make was this:

"Follow thy quest to the end, Huon of Bordeaux, and I shall be rewarded by thy courage, for about you there is much which touches my heart—why, I know not. Save that wise women have foretold that I shall come to have a sword-brother and cup-mate of mortal birth and mayhap thou are that man. Go now without fear, for naught within the bounds of this forest will harm you and your road is plain to follow."

Before Huon could make answer Oberon and his knights were gone, disappearing into the dark of the forest where they were swallowed up as if they had never been. Huon and his companions then got to horse and rode on along the path which Oberon had pointed out to them. And at length they came out of the Fairy wood into a land of meadows and streams.

When they were free of the forest Huon's men began to talk among themselves of the gifts their lord now carried. And some of them said that mayhap it was only a spell laid upon them in the Fairy wood which made such marvels seem to be. But out in these fields Oberon's power was naught and neither horn nor cup would obey their master. So did they talk and talk until Huon grew angered and wearied at their unbelief. And, thinking to put a stop to their clacking tongues, he raised the horn and blew a deep blast.

Above them the sky clouded darkly and from the ground before them there shot up to these gloomy heavens a pillar of green flames from the heart of which burst forth Oberon and his Elf knights, shields before them and naked, burning swords in their hands.

"Where stands your enemy?" shouted Oberon and all the field rang with his cry.

Then was Huon ashamed of what he had done and fearful in his heart of what the Fairy King would say concerning his foolishness. But he dismounted from his charger and came humbly to stand before Oberon to confess his fault.

Oberon's face flushed with anger and his green eyes were as coals of wrath within his head. But when Huon had confessed with manly readiness the full sum of his foolishness the Fairy King shook his head sadly and replied:

"Alas, Huon, many and grave are the dangers before you and deep will be your sorrow before you finish with this task.

So put aside these childish follies lest you fare so ill that even I cannot bring you free. Use not the horn again unless you stand in such peril as you can see of it no easement but death. Or else I shall take back my gift and leave you to perish after your own foolish fashion!"

Huon did then swear by the Cross that never again would he use the gifts lightly, but rather would he guard them with his life. And Oberon and his knights retired into the pillar of flame and so were gone.

But Huon and those who followed him rode on through the countryside until against the sky the walls and towers of a city were to be seen. There they determined to spend the night.

X. WHICH TELLETH OF THE CITY OF TORMONT AND WHAT CHANCED THEREIN

WHEN THE KNIGHTS of France came nigh unto the gates of the strange city a voice called out to them, saying:

"By the crosses which ye bear so boldly limned upon thy shields ye be Christian men. Fly hence, and that speedily, if ye would keep life within thy bodies—for this be the City of Tormont and our lord is one Macaire who hath a great and burning hate for all Christians and hath sworn that all who fall into his hands shall be short of a head!"

But Huon called in answer:

"Night is full upon us and we seek shelter. Nor do we have any fear of your dread lord. Unbar the gate that we may enter into Tormont."

So did it pass that they came into the city and on the other side of the gates they found awaiting them he who had warned them—Gonder, Steward of Tormont, an honest man. And when he saw that they could not be persuaded to flee beyond the wrath of Macaire he urged them to go with him to his own dwelling where they might yet be safe.

Now Tormont was a city of fine houses and tall towers, but

within her streets was a great multitude of beggars and sore
was their state so that Huon and his companions felt much
pity for them. And Huon asked of Gonder why so many
suffered thus. The Steward replied that it was by the will of
Lord Macaire who was deep in all manner of wickedness.

When they came into Gonder's house Huon took from his
belt a purse of gold and gave it into the Steward's hands,
saying:

"Taking this and go into the market place, there buying all
meat and bread, such as is necessary for a feast. Then have
hither all these men and women who beg in the streets and
give them to eat, so that tonight no one within Tormont
will go hungry to bed."

Gonder did as Huon bade him. And from all the ways of
Tormont came the beggars to eat of the food set out for
them. Huon then did bring out the magic cup and passed it
among all that company. To everyone who ate there it was
full of its bounty and to none did it stand empty. So merry
indeed was the feasting.

As the hour waxed late Huon took from his neck the chain
of the Fairy horn and gave the wondrous gift into Gonder's
keeping with these words:

"Take thou this horn and treasure it well, that it may not
be lost no matter how merry we become. For it is the chief
of all my holdings and it must not be taken from me."

Gonder did hang the horn about his own neck and swear
to Huon that he would hold it from all harm.

Now Macaire, the Lord of Tormont, sent into the market
place the servants of his palace to buy meat for his table.
Shortly they did return to him saying that there was no meat
left to be boughten, for a stranger had purchased it all for
a feast to be given to the city beggars. And even now all
the poor of the town were eating it in the house of Gonder.

Much astonished at such tidings Macaire thought that he
must see for himself this outlander who was feeding the
beggars of Tormont. So he did put on him a long cloak of
dusty black, such as the poorest of the town did wear, and,
with his knights, he went down into the town. Leaving his
men without in the street, he went into Gonder's house and

seated himself humbly at one of the far tables, looking about him slyly at all that passed.

Now it chanced that shortly after the Lord of Tormont crept in among them, Huon came to the table where Macaire had seated himself, bearing the Fairy cup which he offered to all who sat there. But when the cup came into Macaire's grasp and he raised it to drink—lo—the wine was gone and he held only an empty cup!

"What manner of man art thou?" cried Huon. "For no honest man does this cup go dry!" Reaching forth his hand he pulled from Macaire's head the hood of his beggar's cloak.

And Gonder shouted: "He is Macaire, Lord of Tormont!"

Before they could lay hand upon him Macaire rushed to the street door and called to his men to come and take these outlanders. But Huon and the other French knights were not to be so easily captured. They fought their way out and through the crowded streets until they won to a strong watchtower which stood in the very heart of Tormont. There they did set upon the few guardsmen at its portal and put them to the sword, thus gaining the protection of strong walls.

Outside this tower Macaire gathered all the might of Tormont, thinking that in time hunger and thirst would drive its defenders into his hands. Huon saw that this might come, for there was no escape from this hold save through the forces drawn up against them.

Then did Duke Garyn urge him thus:

"Sound now the horn which King Oberon did give you—for this is so great a peril that he will grant your call a rightful one."

Huon put his hand to his breast and in that moment recollected that he had given the horn into Gonder's keeping and had it not. When he told this to the others they did reproach him for his great folly and he answered them not, for he knew that what they said to him was true.

But meanwhile Gonder remembered the horn and how this stranger, now pent within the watchtower, had said that it was the chief of his treasures. So he determined to take it to him, since secretly in his heart Gonder hated the Lord Macaire for the many evils he had wrought.

He went openly to Macaire and said:

"Lord, let me go and speak unto these outlanders. Since they trust me, mayhap I can counsel them into surrender by pointing out in what dire straits they now lie."

Macaire agreed, for he was minded to win the tower with as little bloodshed as possible and these strangers had already proved themselves stout warriors.

XI. HOW HUON DID CALL UP THE ELF KNIGHTS AND OF THE DOOM OF MACAIRE

GONDER WENT openly to the gate of the watchtower, unarmed and bearing no weapons, but carrying in his hands a scarf of white silk that those within might know that he came in peace. At Huon's order the way was unbarred and he came in, to address the Lord from Bordeaux thus:

"Macaire will have they heads from thy shoulders if ye surrender to him, therefore listen not to any promises which he may make thee, for they will be as false as river quicksand which entrapeth the traveler to his doom. Ye can expect no mercy from him and I can truly see naught before ye but death. But I have brought hither this horn which ye did entrust to me, saying that it was the greatest of thy treasures."

Huon fairly snatched the magic horn from Gonder, crying aloud:

"Good Steward, with this horn you have brought us our deliverance, as you and all of Tormont shall now see!"

And putting horn to lip he blew such a blast as echoed from the towers and walls of all the city, into the very heart of Heaven itself. With that sounding came a wind like unto the tempest they had known in the wood of Fairy.

A sword of fire clove the sky above Tormont and out of that light came the bat-winged horses of the Hills ridden by Oberon's forces. Each Elf knight's sword swung loose in his hand and as they rode down the wind into the city they cried aloud the battle cries of their own world which lies beyond the rim of mortal earth.

At this dread sight those who followed Macaire were greatly afeared and some fled. But others, of a stronger breed, stood fast. And Huon and his men issued forth to do battle with these.

Then began such a clamor as was never before heard upon this earth. Red streams of brave men's blood did fill the gutters of the streets and bodies lay within every doorway and upon every threshold. For there was no stopping the vengeance of the Elf knights. Nor were the men of France behind them in the harrowing of Tormont. Mighty were the deeds done by Huon and Garyn and Gerames and those who followed them.

At long last there remained none in the whole city to stand against them. And chief among the slain lay Macaire who, evil though his life had been, fought valiantly against all comers and did not fall until the very end of the battle. So did Huon mourn that so brave a man had lived so ill.

When Tormont was cleansed of this false lord and those who had done his wicked will, Oberon came to Huon and said:

"As we promised, we came to your aid and now this city has fallen and lies within your hand to do with as you will. What is your plan for Tormont?"

Huon looked upon this once fair city now torn and brought to deep suffering through battle, and he considered before he answered.

"Tormont I do not want, nor do I think that any of those in my train will wish to reign here, so far from our native land. Therefore let Gonder, who is an honest man, rule as Tormont's lord. And we shall go our way."

All those with Huon agreed and thus did the Steward Gonder become Lord of Tormont. And so well and long did he rule that in later years Tormont became one of the greatest cities of the Saracen land, to the glory of its people. But never more did Huon or those with him behold its towers again.

Rather did they go out into the countryside where Oberon and his Elf knights bid them farewell, only first did the Fairy King lay upon Huon another warning, namely:

"So far upon your quest have you come without hurt and may it so continue with you. But I fear that it will not be so for long, for you are a rash youth and have little knowledge of the world. Forget not this warning which I give you now, for your remembrance of it will mean much good or ill in the future. Speak always the full truth and let no manner of falsehood pass your lips. For if you lie you will lose my aid and, be your need ever so great, I shall not come to you."

Huon swore loudly that he would do as Oberon wished, that no falsehood would he utter. But the Fairy King still looked with sorrow upon him as if he saw ill coming in the future.

Before he went out from the mortal world Oberon raised up out of the wilderness a fine pavilion to house all the French company, and brought out of the air by his magic a goodly banquet for their feasting.

Now many among them nured deep wounds taken in the fighting and when Huon saw their plight he said:

"Since this quest was laid upon me only, I shall ride alone to its finish. Stay you here and tend your hurts until I come again. But if I come not within the next waxing and waning of the moon, count me as one dead and bear back to Bordeaux the story of our faring."

They all cried out against this, but Huon would not listen to their hot protests. Then, at last, Gerames said:

"Before you now lies the Castle of Dunother where dwells the Giant Angalafar. Take another road and avoid this one danger."

But when Huon had bade them all be of good cheer and farewell, he chose the road to Dunother, being minded to see the famed hold of the Giant Angalafar.

XII. HOW HUON FARED AT CASTLE DUNOTHER

DUNOTHER AROSE gray and grim from a barren plain. From its stark towers no banners flew and there was about it an air of ill omen, so that Huon was half-minded to ride by it. Only to his ears there sounded a regular thud-thudding noise for which he could see no source until he came, drawn by curiosity, to the gate.

There stood, on either side of the portal, two giants fashioned of steel and brass by a skill which was that of no mortal man. In the hands of these giants rested thick clubs of iron and with these clubs they beat the ground before the gate so that nothing might pass through and escape horrible death. Huon watched for a long time but he could see no instant when one or the other of the clubs was not in motion.

As he so watched he heard a voice call to him and, lifting his eyes to the tower above the gate, he saw in a window there a damsel of much beauty and few years. She did cry upon him to wait, and shortly after the giants ceased their pounding so that Huon might ride through the now open gate to the courtyard where the damsel stood awaiting him.

When he did dismount and come to her she did weep most piteously and cling to him, saying:

"Oh, gentle lord, for seven years no mortal man has ridden hither in answer to my prayers—so have I served a loathly giant as handmaiden without hope of succor. I pray you, free me from this fate. Know you I am Sebylle, once a maiden of high degree in the kingdom of France. But my father did choose to come to this foul land upon a holy pilgrimage. And while he was so gone from me, my lady mother died and I was left desolate. So did I determine to follow my father. But when I came into this country I found no man who could tell me of him. And then the caravan with which I journeyed was overwhelmed by Angalafar. The men he killed at once, but he had never before sighted a Christian maid. So he brought me hither where I am a serving wench in his household."

Huon's anger quickened as he heard her tale and he promised in his heart that he would have the life of Angalafar for the way he had served a maid of France. So when the maiden came to herself and urged him to leave before the Giant returned, he refused all her pleas.

"You will only meet your death because of your stubbornness," she told him sorrowfully. "For Angalafar hath a suit of mail which cannot be riven by any lance or sword forged by man. Wearing it he cannot be conquered. Nor can another man put it on him save by Angalafar's own wish. As long as he lives will that be so."

When Huon heard this he thirsted greatly for that suit of mail and vowed that he would have it from Angalafar, to serve him even as it had served the Giant for many years. But the maiden began to mourn as if Huon were already dead before her eyes and reproached him with his stubbornness in not fleeing Dunother before Angalafar returned.

Bidding her be of good heart Huon lingered through the day, eating of the fine meats the damsel served him and drinking the wine from his magic cup. And in the cool of the evening Angalafar returned to the castle, a whole ox held beneath his arm as one might carry a pet hare.

Truly a fearsome sight was this monster, being more than thirty feet tall and having the tusks of a wild boar to serve him as teeth. But he was in a good humor because of the ox, so that when Huon came boldly out before him he did not smite him instantly but rather roared at him the questions of who was he and why had he come to Dunother.

Huon replied without fear, cheerily enough.

"It is told through this land that you do keep such a suit of mail as no mortal man has seen—since it holds its wearer safe from all attack. I am Huon of Bordeaux, a knight of the realm of France, who has journeyed hither to see this marvel."

Angalafar was pleased with this answer and he brought forth from a chest a suit of mail which shone as if each link within its fashioning had been cut from gold or silver.

"Look well," he said to Huon, "for this will be your last

sight upon earth, since I intend to put a speedy end to you—"

But Huon allowed no part of the wonder he felt within him to show upon his face. Rather did he strive to look most coldly upon the mail as he said:

"So this poor, small thing be that boast of Dunother? Faith, by Our Lord, I have seen better in my own armory of Bordeaux. It is too small to even cover my shoulders!"

Now at these slighting words Angalafar was greatly wroth and in his anger he lost the keenness of his wit, for he cried out:

"Put it on thy back, outlander, and see whether or no it will fit across thy puny boy's shoulders!"

With a high heart Huon did as Angalafar bid and never had a coat of mail fit him so well. Light it was as the silk of Cathay and yet as strong as a brand forged by the olden gods. When he stood full armed Angalafar demanded:

"Do you not find this now the finest mail you have ever known?"

"True," replied Huon, drawing his sword. "So fine is this mail that I do wish it to be mine hereafter. I thank thee right heartily, Angalafar, for so princely a gift."

Then did Angalafar perceive how he had been tricked and, with a bellow of rage, he struck at Huon with his ax. But the stroke fell upon the coat of mail and to the knight it was but the buffet of a feather. So it was with all the blows which the Giant showered upon him until at last, missing his footing in one blind rush, Angalafar fell to the floor of the hall. Huon sprang at the fallen monster and hacked off his head, thus putting an end to the evil life of this leathly giant.

The French knight then called upon the Damsel Sebylle to come forth from her hiding and greatly did she rejoice at the sight of her captor so brought to naught and laid low. To her did Huon then give the Castle of Dunother and all that it contained, so that she, who had been a serving wench, was now a lady of much wealth and wide lands. For himself he did take only the coat of mail which he wore as he rode on into the land of the Saracens toward the dread city of Babylon.

XIII. OF MALABRON THE SEA BEAST, AND THE GIANT AGRAPUT

Now IT CHANCED that across the road to Babylon lay a deep river whereof the waters did rush very swiftly and the dark current did seem to Huon to be a trap. Here was no bridge, nor was there any ford for travelers and the young knight, having upon his back the weight of sword, shield and mail, could see no way of winning through the flood. So he sat down upon the bank and stared into the sullen depths of the stream.

Then before his eyes the waters were troubled as if some great creature strove there. And from the curls of foam arose the naked head and shoulders of a young and comely man. But when the stranger swam most easily to where Huon rested upon the bank, lo, he revealed that a scaled tail served him as lower limbs.

Huon was amazed at such a sight and his surprise was even greater when the river creature hailed him thus:

"Ho, Huon of Bordeaux, knight of France, I am Malabron of the realm of Fairy, sent hither by King Oberon to give you aid."

Then did the knight approach nearer to the flood to point to that long and shining tail which Malabron used with as much ease as Huon used his two legs.

"Art thou man or monster?" the youth from Bordeaux demanded.

Malabron laughed. "Neither, sir knight. I wear this strange guise because I have broken the laws of our immortal world. For a thousand weary years must I bide so within the boundaries of your world and time. And of these years I have served a full nine hundred and fifty. Now shall we consider your straits—Behold, Huon!"

With those words Malabron did clap together his hands,

making a loud sound which could be heard even above the roaring of the river. And straightway there came from out of the water itself a fine boat well made and cleverly fashioned to withstand the beating of the water.

Into this Huon did lead his charger, although the beast did rebel against such travel and needs must be constrained to it with many soothing words. Once the knight and his mount were safe aboard, Malabron did grasp with his white teeth the rope which was fastened to the bow. And faster than any mortal might, he swam through the river waters, towing behind him the boat. So was Huon brought to the far side of the river.

When he had disembarked from the boat he thanked Malabron. But the fish-man shook his head against such words, saying in turn:

"Nay, thank me not, Huon of Bordeaux. For by this service to you have I won fifty years remittance from my exile. Now am I free to return to my own land. So rather be my thanks yours. When we meet again I shall be in my proper place among King Oberon's lords. Therefore, all manner of good luck be yours for this day's work and may you have the good fortune you deserve!"

With that Malabron sank into the stream and was gone, although Huon called upon him twice or thrice, being ill at ease alone in this strange and desolate land. For by crossing the river he had come into a desert where there seemed to be no other living thing.

But ere he had ridden a full half league he came across footprints in the sand. And so large were these prints that he knew no living man but a giant or monster had made them. Thus he was not surprised to find, upon riding around the edge of a bare rock cliff, a giant sitting in the sand and whetting a twelve-foot sword on a stone.

Now this was the Giant Agraput who was brother to that same Angalafar whom Huon had slain. And when he saw Huon he recognized the coat of mail which the knight wore. So did he take the young man to be some messenger sent by his brother. And he called to Huon in such a voice as rang from the cliffs like a war trumpet:

"How does my brother, Angalafar? And why has he sent you hither?"

Huon made answer as best he might, saying:

"Angalafar bides quietly at Dunother (which was the truth for he lay at peace in a courtyard grave there) and I ride for Babylon."

But of his mission he said nothing since he could not speak the truth and he held in mind Oberon's warning against uttering that which was false.

"Good indeed is it then that Fate has brought us to this meeting," boomed Agraput, "for I am held in high fear in those parts and, since my brother has given you his fine coat of mail to wear, I can do no less than to give you this." And he tossed to Huon a ring of red gold which he pulled from his finger and which was so large that the knight needs must set it about his wrist.

"Show that to any who would bar your way at the gates of Babylon. For Gaudys, the Emir of that city, owes me a half year's tribute and you can remind him of that when you are finished with the task my good brother has set you."

Huon promised that he would do as Agraput asked and with the Giant's ring upon his arm he went on his way.

Soon the track he followed led out of this harsh and barren wasteland into a green country where trees of ripening fruit overhung the roads and peasants tilled rich fields. Here did Huon rest the night and ease his mount from weary travel. And he marveled at all that had chanced since he had ridden forth from his keep of Bordeaux. So thinking of his home he did feel the tears rise to his eyes and he knew the pain of an aching heart. For he longed to see once more his gentle mother, the good Duchess Aclis (not knowing that now she lay in her deep tomb) and his brother Gerard who was even then ruling Bordeaux with a stern and heavy hand.

XIV. HOW HUON SPAKE FALSELY AND THE EVIL THAT CAME TO HIM THEREFOR

WEARING THE armor of Angalafar and the ring which was Agraput's, Huon came to the gates of Babylon. To the first guardsman he did show the ring, saying naught lest speech betray him as a stranger to this land, and so great was the fear of Agraput in the city that he was passed freely through the portal. But when he came to a second gate the sentry there raised a spear against him and bade him tell who he was and from whence he came.

The French knight replied shortly that he was one Huon and that he had weighty business with the Emir Gaudys. Then he also held forth his wrist that the sentry might see the Giant's ring. The Saracen did bow low but still held his place barring the road, saying:

"The Giant Agraput is indeed a great lord and much esteemed by our Emir. But those who serve him are many and not always of our kind. This is a high feast day for the followers of the Prophet and no unbeliever must lie within our walls at this time. So I must ask you, stranger, are you of our true faith?"

Huon, being impatient and wishful to win into the city, answered quickly, "Aye."

Nor was it until he was within the walls of Babylon that he bethought himself that he had spoken that which was false. So was he in some unease of mind, remembering how Oberon had so sternly warned him against that sin. But he comforted himself with the belief that his fault had come through impatience and not because he had willed to err and he hoped that for such an excuse the Fairy King would not forsake him.

However, at that moment King Oberon, sitting at ease in his court, cried aloud so that his chief lord Gloriant asked if he felt some pang. And Oberon made sorrowful answer thus:

"Aye, deep into my heart has struck a spear of pain, for that youth, Huon of Bordeaux, whom I love as a brother, hath broken his pledged word. With black falsehood upon his lips has he ridden into Babylon. And there he is fated to fall into such danger as will claim his life. So shall he call upon me for aid in his extremity, but I cannot go to him. Unless Our Lord Jesu Himself hold out His Hand, Huon be sped!"

And so great was his grief that he went out from the company of his lords and abode alone, weeping, for many hours' space.

But in Babylon Huon rode on to the Emir's palace, no man saying him nay, for all saw Agraput's ring and thought the young knight to be the Giant's rightful messenger.

Now Gaudys had spread a feast for all comers, since he was minded that day to betroth his daughter Claramonde to the Dey of Hircania. Upon his right hand was the Dey seated and there was much mirth and joy among the company—until Huon did enter, his shield ready upon his shoulder, his unsheathed sword in his hand. All marveled to see an armed man come into them as if he sought some sworn enemy there. But the Emir, seeing the ring about the youth's wrist, thought him the messenger of Agraput whom all there feared and he arose to bid the stranger courteous welcome.

Only, before he could speak the words which lay upon his tongue, Huon did tread lightly to the side of Claramonde and, raising her up from her seat, did kiss her full upon her lips even as Charlemagne had ordered him.

Then he turned quickly and, with his naked sword, he smote off the head of the Dey so that it rolled across the feast table to the very fingers of Gaudys.

"Villain! What foul mischief is this?" shouted the Emir. "Who art thou to dare such a deed?"

"I am Huon of Bordeaux, knight and peer of France, and liege man to King Charlemagne. My lord has laid upon me this task, that I must kiss upon the mouth your fair daughter, strike from his shoulders the head of the most noble lord at your table, and take a fistful of hair from your beard and five of your great teeth!"

At first the Emir thought Huon a mad man, but when

the Frenchman stretched forth his hand to seize upon Gaudys' beard, the Emir cried aloud for his guard to overpower the stranger. Now did Huon raise the horn of Oberon and blow so deep a blast that the sound rang in the ears of all the city. But no clouds gathered in answer, no lightning flashed, no Elf knights rode the steeds of storm. And Huon knew that his falsehood was held against him. So he threw the horn from him, crying:

"Small was my fault, King Oberon, born of thoughtless folly rather than of willful evil. But if now I am doomed to fall beneath the swords of these Saracens, may you long remember how you left me to my death!"

Then, with his shield before him and his sword swinging in his hand, he did fight most valiantly. But, at last, by sheer weight of numbers, was he overcome. Swiftly was he bound and taken to a deep dungeon, there left in chains to starve by the will of Gaudys.

But the Lady Claramonde was troubled in her heart and went to her couch that night uneasy in mind and body, thinking much of Huon's fair youth and his great comeliness which was such as few maidens could be indifferent to. And, since she had secretly hated the old Dey of Hircania, who had been her father's friend and not hers, she felt most kindly toward the man who had rid her of such a husband. So sleep came not and she turned many times upon her pillows, until she could no longer lie there. She arose and put on a long cloak of black so that in the shadows of the night no one could mark her passing.

Taking with her a small basket of meat and bread and a jar of water, she stole down the hundred dark steps into the dungeons of the Emir. There she did pacify the stupid sentry with a gold piece so that he unbarred the door of Huon's cell that she might look upon the notable captive. Secretly she gave to the prisoner the food and drink, and he thought that surely within the whole mortal world there was nowhere else so fair or kind a maiden.

And then was the great love between these two born. And of that love came much sorrow and much joy for both—as is the way of love between man and maid.

XV. HOW GAUDYS WAS OVERBORNE AND HUON GAINED HIS HEART'S DESIRE

WHILE HUON LAY so pent in his foul prison, those who had followed him from France and those who loved him well, namely Duke Garyn and the Knight Gerames, grew fearful of his fate. For Huon returned not to them at the time he had appointed. Instead of taking ship for France as their leader had ordered them to do, they decided to ride on toward Babylon that they might gain news of him.

When they came nigh to the Saracen city Gerames said to Duke Garyn:

"Do you and these other knights and squires remain here well hid, for no man in this land looking upon you would not know you for outlanders. But I have lived here for many years and if I put on the clothing of a desert chieftain none will learn my disguise is false. So clad I can win into the very court of the Emir and discover how it has fared there with Huon, good or ill."

To this plan the Duke Garyn did agree, seeing the wisdom of it. And Gerames did put on him the robes of a desert chieftain and rode alone through the gates of Babylon.

He went into the court of the Emir, telling the sentries that he was an envoy sent to Babylon by the Caliph Ivoryn, who was full brother to Gaudys. This did delight the Emir exceedingly, for he had long been wishful to have tidings from his brother. And he had Gerames brought to him, showing him all manner of honor and ordering a feast to be given to celebrate his coming to the city.

Now as they sat eating and drinking Gerames began cunningly to talk of feats of arms and of the mighty warriors he had known and of their skill in battle. Until at length Gaudys said:

"Aye, mighty indeed were these men of whom you have spoken so well. But there was a dog of a Christian who, within this very room, held off half my guards before he could be pulled down."

At these words Gerames' heart leaped within his breast for he knew that Gaudys spoke of Huon. And he demanded to know what had become of so brave a warrior.

"He lies beneath my dunghill," returned Gaudys. "For when neither food nor drink was given him, he did as all mortals do—left this world and his body speedily enough. And so we are well rid of him!"

Then was Gerames cast down. And he thought that all he had now to live for was revenge upon this Emir who had served Huon so cruelly, even to the boy's death. But of his thoughts he spoke none aloud.

When the feast was done and it was late at night, the Lady Claramonde did creep forth from her chamber with meat and drink hid beneath her cloak. And, as she passed along the dark halls, Gerames sighted her. Wondering at her employ he followed her, even into the dungeon where Huon lay.

And, seeing the youth still living, a mighty cry of joy burst from Gerames' throat, afrighting the lady and greatly astonishing Huon. But when the old knight threw aside the hood of his cloak and Huon knew that he was the faithful Gerames, the young man rejoiced.

Swiftly he did tell Gerames how the Lady Claramonde had saved him from death by starvation and had persuaded the jailer to set out the body of a prisoner, dead from the fever, as Huon's own, so that all the court believed him dead and buried.

Each night had Claramonde urged him with many tears and lamentations to flee Babylon. But without the teeth and hair of Gaudys he would not go. And so had it been to the coming of Gerames.

Having heard the lady's pleas and the firm refusal of Huon, Gerames asked why the young knight had not asked help from King Oberon. Red then with shame was Huon's face and low hung his head as he made true confession of his sin of falsehood.

"Hard has been your lot since that hour and much has

been your suffering," mused Gerames. "Who knows what lies within the mind of the Elf King? Were you to freely acknowledge your fault and ask humbly for pardon—mayhap he would come to do you service once more. In the hall of the Emir now hangs that horn which was taken from you. Come, let us take it once more. And if we fail we shall fall at the sword's point, which is fair enough ending for any belted knight!"

Thus heartened by Gerames' words they crept forth into the hall of the Emir and Huon lifted down the silver horn. But ere he could set it to lip, there burst upon them divers members of the guard. Gerames leapt out with unsheathed sword to ward off the attack, shouting:

"Sound the horn! And if it be Our Lord's will let King Oberon answer!"

Out rang the blast of the horn, its notes reaching to high Heaven and to the depths of Hell, so that all who heard, mortal or spirit, were shaken. Nor could Oberon hold fast against that summoning, for he who blew did so with a humble and contrite heart.

So did the hosts of Fairy descend upon Babylon and those who dared to stand against them were slain. But those who begged for mercy were spared the sword.

In the hall Huon strove shield to shield with Gaudys. Nor was the fight an easy one, for Gaudys was a mighty man of arms, renowned through all the width of the Saracen lands. And Huon trod warily, the bright sparks of fire flying from his armor under the blows of the Emir.

But in the end Huon, with one last strong blow, brought down the Emir of Babylon and from the fallen man's jaw did he smite out the white teeth, from his chin he cut the wiry beard.

And these hairs and teeth Oberon did place within a golden box which he gave unto Gerames, ordering him to guard them with his life until they came again into the court of Charlemagne.

XVI. HOW HUON RETURNED TO FRANCE AND GERARD PLOTTED EVIL

HAVING GAINED the teeth and beard of Gaudys and otherwise fulfilled the quest Charlemagne had set him, Huon and his followers now took ship for Rome. And there, by the Holy Father himself, was the young knight wed to Claramonde. Now Huon was impatient to reach Bordeaux once more and, chancing to hear of a ship bound for France, he took passage on it for himself, his Lady, and Gerames. As the ship was a small one there was no place aboard her for the other knights and squires of his train and they decided to return to France by marching over land, the longer way.

Now when Huon had safely come again to a French port he sent a swift messenger to Bordeaux to tell Gerard of his homecoming. And out of that act came much sorrow for Huon and his fair lady.

For all these months when Huon had been swallowed up in the land of the Saracens, Gerard had deemed him dead and had had himself proclaimed Duke and overlord of Bordeaux. In this wickedness was he upheld by Gylberde, the father of his wife and as black a villain as ever trod the fields of France.

When Huon's messenger came to the keep of Bordeaux, Gerard knew the keen bite of fear, for he believed that his brother would be greatly wroth with him when he discovered how ill matters had gone with the duchy. So Gerard sent the messenger into a private room and stationed a guard before the door thereof so that none might have word with the man. But Gerard himself hastened to Gylberde for counsel.

Gylberde was also frightened, for he had not dealt justly with certain men of Bordeaux and there would be many voices raised against him should Huon return to rule there. So he spoke in this wise to Gerard:

"All this land knows the heat of your brother's anger and

the heaviness of his hand when he has cause to raise it against any man. If he comes again to Bordeaux surely he will not deal softly with you—since there will be full many to sing aloud fancied wrongs. Also, if he is again Duke of Bordeaux, you will be only a landless nothing without a place to lay your head—"

At those words the Lady Roselyn, she who was wife to Gerard and daughter to Gylberde, lifted her voice in loud argument, saying that she had not wed to share a beggar's couch and crust, and that Gerard dared not use her so but must keep her Lady Duchess of Bordeaux. Mightily did she rage and employ all her wiles until her husband was fain to give into his two hands the moon itself if she would only cease. So he turned to Gylberde for the second time and demanded what he must do to keep Huon from Bordeaux.

"Time has not cooled the ire of King Charlemagne against your brother nor in any way has his heart been softened. And is it not true that the doom he laid upon Huon, should he rashly return without fulfilling the quest, was death? Therefore, do you go secretly to Huon, taking with you no squire or other outrider, since the fewer tongues which may speak of this the better. Discover from Huon's own lips how matters stand with him.

"If he has truly accomplished that which the King ordered him to do—then lead him home by the lower road in the east valley and there I shall lie in wait with my men to take him and those with him captive. We will bring them here to the keep of Bordeaux, traveling by night so that no one along the way may see who it is we hold in bonds. And here shall we keep them close until such a time as we can decide what is to be done."

To this plot Gerard agreed willingly enough, so lost to all good had his envy and the power of his wife made him, and he did just as Gylberde urged. Without knight or squire he stole out of the city and rode to that abbey where Huon, his lady wife, and Gerames were resting. Nor did Gylberde linger in Bordeaux but hurried forth on another track with a goodly band of desperate men who were sworn to obey him in all things.

As Gerard came into the courtyard of the abbey Huon ran forth to greet him joyfully, embracing his brother and calling down all manner of good fortune upon the younger man, saying:

"Not the least of the blessings which Our Lord hath granted me is this meeting with you, my dear brother. Tell me, how does our mother? Why comes she not with you?"

Then did Gerard hang his head low, for, villain though he now was, he had greatly loved the Duchess Aclis and it hurt him deeply to speak of her death as he must. And when Huon heard how that noble lady had been stricken down at the tale of his misfortunes at court, he was in turn as one smitten dumb and could only gaze pitifully into the shifting eyes of Gerard.

Beneath that piteous appeal Gerard moved unhappily as might an ox threatened with a goad, and he hastened to ask concerning the success of his brother's mission. Absent were Huon's replies for his thoughts were still with the Duchess Aclis. But from his halting words Gerard learned that the news was as ill as his fears had painted it. Huon had performed the task set him by the King and was even now about to ride to court with the proof.

So Gerard hastened to suggest that he join Huon's small party, so he might witness his brother's triumph at court. Huon agreed, but with a heavy heart, for it would be a triumph emptied now of all joy.

By Gerard's urging they rode forth on the valley road, Huon and Gerames mounted on war chargers and Claramonde riding upon a strong white mule. But ere they had gone a league beyond the abbey walls, they were attacked by Gylberde and his men. And, when Huon saw even his brother's sword turned against him, he lost heart, threw away his weapons and allowed himself to be taken. So did Huon enter again his city of Bordeaux, not triumphantly before the faces of his people, but secretly at night, bound to the saddle of his own horse. And with him rode Gerames and Claramonde in like distress.

But Gerard was on his way to the King's court with a black plan in his traitor heart.

XVII. HOW HUON STOOD IN GREAT PERIL AND GERAMES SUMMONED OBERON FOR THE LAST TIME

GERARD CAME TO the court of King Charlemagne and there spake aloud before all the company, saying:

"Lord King, it was thy will long months ago to lay upon my brother, Huon, a perilous quest—namely to go into Babylon of the Saracens and there smite off the head of the chief man who sat upon the right hand of the Emir, to lay upon the mouth of the Emir's daughter a free kiss, and to take as tribute from Gaudys himself a handful of beard and five of his teeth. These was he to bring hither to hold before your eyes in token of his deeds. But, unless he accomplish this, he was not to return to the realm of France unless he wished to part speedily with his head and his life."

King Charlemagne nodded. "Even as you have said, it is so. But why do you recall to our minds on this day the punishment of that traitor who doubtless long since was meat for crows?"

Then did Gerard yield to the blackness in his heart and made answer in this wise:

"Not so, Lord King. At this very hour Huon lies in the keep of Bordeaux awaiting thy pleasure. And whatsoever thou dost order—the same shall be done unto him!"

At this cruel speech several of the lords and peers did grow red and white in the face with shame—to hear brother so denounce brother to sure and sudden death. And amongst these was that Duke Naymes who had once stood good friend to Huon and was now determined to fight for him again. So that now he did speak out quickly.

"Mayhap Huon hath done as he was bade and was returning to report his deeds," he began.

But Gerard interrupted him in great haste.

"Nay. Knowing that no living man might perform such

acts as the King ordered, he but kept beyond the borders of France until he hoped that the memory of his foul deeds had grown dim in all men's minds. Then did he venture back secretly, trusting that I would prove as false a rogue as he and give him shelter against the just wrath of the King. But instead I have put him in ward and have ridden hither to know the King's will."

Now in these months Charlemagne's wrath against Huon had grown no less or lighter and, when Gerard had done, he thundered forth that Huon was to die a traitor's death as soon as possible.

But Naymes, and those other peers who thought shame of this business, cried aloud that Huon should not be so cruelly used without a hearing. And as they spake so strongly, with flashing eyes and flushed cheeks, the King was forced to their will and agreed to journey to Bordeaux where Huon lay in prison, there hear the unfortunate youth's own story.

And so the court went to Bordeaux and this was to the liking of neither Gerard nor Gylberde, who feared that by some trick of fate Huon would win free of the trap they had set for him.

In Bordeaux, Huon, the Lady Claramonde, and the faithful Gerames were brought out of prison into the light of day and piteous it was to see their hard plight. Many there were among the lords of the court who said privately to one another that there seemed to be little evil in these three.

Then one Gaulter, a knight of mean degree and distantly kin to Gylberde, arose to demand that Huon suffer the full penalty of the law. And to this plea Gylberde nodded happy assent. Gerard would have spoken likewise but, with his brother's eyes upon him, he could make no sound and his lying words were thrust back into his throat until he thought himself nigh strangled by them. So he said nothing, but of him only did Huon seem aware. And when the youth spoke it was directly to his false brother.

"Know you, when our lord king laid upon me this heavy task I did go out of France to His Holiness, the Pope, in Rome. And with his holy blessing I sailed unto the shores of that land which is thrall to the Saracen host."

Then did he relate all those adventures and misadventures which had befallen him—even as are set down in this chronicle. And all those hearing marveled at his tale which was strange indeed to their ears.

When Huon had done he looked away from Gerard for the first time, holding up his head to face the King fully, even as an honest man would stand. And so he waited for the verdict of Charlemagne.

But Gylberde, fearing the sympathy which the tale had aroused in the court, shouted:

"If this villain speaks true—where is the beard and where are the teeth of Gaudys? Let him show them now."

Huon turned again to Gerard and spake sorrowfully:

"Nay, I have them not. They were wrested from the good Sir Gerames by you, my brother. If all love be not wholly dead between us, I pray you now, bring forth the casket that I may not be foresworn before the lords of France."

But Gerard stirred not, although within him he was sick and faint with terror. For that evil which he had surrendered to held him fast in this last hour when he might have redeemed his soul—held him hard fast in his allegiance to the Ruler of Darkness whose vassal he had become.

And when Gerard did not answer that petition, Huon uttered a moan of sadness and covered his face with his hands as if he could no longer bear to look upon his brother. But Gerames, seeing Huon so stricken, acted for him. And from the young knight's belt he plucked the horn of Oberon, to put it to his lips and blow. And that bugling seemed to rift apart both the hall in which they stood and the sky above it.

XVIII. OF THE TRIUMPH OF HUON AND THE FAIR PROMISE OF OBERON

OUT OF THE riven sky there did descend to the earth of France, even into the city of Bordeaux, Oberon, King and Liege Lord of Fairyland, together with those Fairy lords and Elf knights who did him service.

King Charlemagne and his peers stood dumbstruck at such a sight. And no man dared to move as Oberon put forth his sword and touched those chains which bound Huon, his lady, and Gerames.

Straightway those chains were as dust and the rising wind puffed them away so the three were free, no man putting out hand against them. Gerard and Gylberde were sore afraid at this sight and their limbs shook with their terror, for none might know the will of the Fairy lord or what punishment he would lay upon those who had harmed his friends.

But Oberon clapped together his naked hands and at that sharp sound there came to Huon, through the air, that gold box containing the beard and teeth of Gaudys. And this coffer Oberon bade him open that all there might see that he had faithfully served Charlemagne.

When the King looked upon that coffer and heard all that Huon had undergone, his heart was moved. And Oberon, marking this, spoke sharply:

"Brother King, even as you reign here within the boundaries of France, so do I reign among the People of the Hills in that land which few mortals have ever seen. And since I grow weary of my crown, which is full heavy now as it was not in the days of my youth, I am fain to depart hence, even into Paradise as was promised me centuries ago. The time of my passing is not yet, though the shadow of it lies upon me now. But when I am summoned, then shall I in turn call unto me this youth whom I have proved to be of loyal heart, brave and true beyond the like of most mortals, and he shall be lord over my people and rule forever in the misty valleys and cloud mountains of Elf Land. This do I proclaim before your nobles and mine, and this shall be!"

While they yet marveled at his speech, Oberon leaned far from his saddle and kissed Huon upon the brow as if they were brothers in blood. And so did he also to Claramonde and from that day forward neither did the Duke nor his lady show any mark of age or know any bodily ill. Rather were they possessed of a beauty beyond that of mankind and of eternal youth.

So having laid upon Huon the wardship of his kingdom,

Oberon and his men went out of France, never more to be seen by King Charlemagne and his court. But there were sighs at their going for their like is viewed only once in mayhap a thousand years.

Seeming to stir as if from a dream, the King came again to himself and, looking upon the luckless Gerard, his anger awoke, for he realized that this weak and evil youth and Gylberde would have used the royal power to pull down Huon in order to serve their own ends. Thereupon Charlemagne ordered that these two false knights be dragged away and hung. And no one in all that company raised his voice in their behalf—save only Huon, since he could not forget that Gerard was his brother. But none paid him heed and the King's orders were speedily carried out. So perished these two traitors in the web they had spun for another.

But Huon was named again Duke of Bordeaux and peer of France, and was left to rule in peace, his gentle Duchess by his side.

ADVENTURE THE SECOND

I. HOW HUON WENT FORTH TO BATTLE AND THE LADY CLARAMONDE RECEIVED THE PILGRIMS

ONCE MORE did Duke Huon rule in his city of Bordeaux, and with him sat his fair lady Duchess, in their hearts being much gladness and joy. All the divers counts and lords who were vassal to Huon came then into that city and paid him homage and pledged him faith and loyalty—saving only the Count Angelars.

Now this Angelars was kinsman to that foul traitor Amaury, whom Huon had slain in fair fight before King Charlemagne, and greatly did he hate Huon for that slaying. So now did he fortify his castle and hold it against his rightful lord, swearing that to the Duke he would never render homage while he had life in his body.

And when these rash words were reported to him Huon's anger did wax strong against Angelars. And he summoned into his service such knights and men-at-arms as he knew to be true men and eager for battle. With such in his train he put on that mail which he had won from the Giant Angalafar and took up the sword he had had from his father, the Duke Sevin. Then he sought out Claramonde in her bower, where she rested with all her maidens about her, and spoke to her in this wise:

"My fair lady wife, now do I ride to put to shame this foul traitor Angelars. And while I be gone from Bordeaux do you hold in your two hands the rule of this city. All men shall be servants unto you and your will within these gates shall be as mine."

"Lord Duke," Claramonde made answer, "sad grows my heart to see you with mail girt upon your body and a sword belted about you. For the chances of war are diverse and evil. But if it be your true will to punish this traitor then

I shall say no more. May the Good Lord Jesu hold you ever free from harm and bring you safely back to me. As for Bordeaux, be assured that all shall be done here even as if you yourself sat in the hall of justice from sunrise to sunset."

So did these two part and Huon led his men out of the city toward that keep which Angelars had fortified and held, in defiance of his rightful lord. And there the men of Bordeaux did encompass the castle and begin an assault.

But the same day that Huon did depart out of Bordeaux there came into that city another company of men. And these were pilgrims from Alamayne returning home from the Holy Land where they had visited the Tomb of Our Lord Jesu and looked upon the places where the Prince of Peace had been both quick and dead.

The Lady Claramonde looking forth from the window of her tower chamber saw these pilgrims who were worn and suffering by reason of their long journeying. And she asked what manner of travelers they were. To her was made answer that they were pilgrims newly come from the Holy Land.

So did she then give orders that they be brought into the great hall of the castle and that to them be given meat and drink and new clothing, should they need such. And she herself did go in to serve them with her maids and men. Of this charity came great peril and suffering to Claramonde and those she loved most, as you shall see.

Now the pilgrims rejoiced at the manner of their treatment and as they went on to their own country they ever spoke aloud the praises of the Duchess Claramonde, saying that of all the highborn ladies she was the fairest and best they had ever seen. When they came to their home in Alamayne they met with the Duke Raoul who was their liege lord, this same Raoul being nephew and heir to the Emperor and well beloved by him. But he was a young man of hot passions and took little heed of the rights of lesser men.

And he did ask of the pilgrims the full tale of their wanderings which they did take great pleasure in telling him. Then did the leader of the pilgrims stand forth and say: "Lord Duke, long and far have we journeyed and many and great are the sights we have seen in that journeying. But in our hearts do we cherish the memory of the city of Bordeaux."

"And why do you so?" asked the Duke, amazed, for he did not deem that city of any account.

"Because, Lord Duke, when we came into that city, hungry and weary nigh unto death itself, the Lady Duchess Claramonde, she who is wife to the Duke Huon, did have us into the great hall of the castle. And with her own hands she brought unto us meat and drink and new clothing—if such we needed.

"And of all the ladies we did ever see she is the fairest—even the angels who sit now in the Halls of Heaven might well wish to be fashioned as is she. As she is fair so is she also courteous and in all ways fit to rule. She is duchess in Bordeaux, but she is meet to be a queen in a greater land. Would, Lord Duke, that she might be your wife and so our own dear lady!"

Duke Raoul, hearing this, was fired to see this lady who had so courteously used his people. Many times he thought upon the pilgrim's words until, at length, he knew that he must go even to Bordeaux and look upon the Lady Claramonde with his own eyes. Summoning unto him his chief lords, he made known his will in this wise:

"Since I have heard such things concerning this fair Duchess of Bordeaux I cannot rest in sleep, nor does my meat have any savor in my mouth. I have no lady to share my rule and never had I knowledge before of any who is counted so much a peer among her kind. Therefore I must view this marvel for myself."

Then he did put off his fine robes and his sword. And with stain he blackened his face and let his beard grow upon his chin. So that when he put on him the cloak of a common man he was of rough and poor seeming. In this wise he went to Bordeaux and there he did beg alms at the gate of the castle, saying that he was a pilgrim from the Holy Land.

So the steward, following the orders of his lady, brought him into the great hall where the Duchess sat at meat with all her household. And she received him courteously, giving unto him bread from her own plate. But he could not eat thereof for reason of looking upon her, and he thought that it was true that even Heaven's angels might well wish to appear in the seeming of the Duchess Claramonde.

Then he did know a great longing and love for her which was like a fire lit within him, and he did swear privately that he would have her to wife or die. For he deemed Huon a small lordling of little account whom he could easily dispose of. And with these thoughts making evil and black his heart he departed again for his own land.

II. HOW THE DUKE RAOUL DID PLOT AND OF HUON'S ANSWER THERETO

HAVING SET HIS heart upon gaining the Lady Claramonde to wife, Duke Raoul straightway rode unto the court of his uncle, the Emperor of Alamayne. And the Emperor rejoiced to see his nephew, coming to embrace him and do him all honor before those assembled there, saying:

"My dear kinsman, joyful are we to give you welcome. And if we can in any way serve you, you have but to make known your wishes here."

The Duke Raoul knelt before the Emperor in most humble seeming and paid him homage, before he spoke aloud what was in his mind and what he had been planning since he looked upon the face of the Lady Claramonde.

"Sire, many knights ride in your train and sit in your halls, owing you liege service and all fidelity. Mayhap these be the most skillful and best warriors of all Christendom. It is in my mind that if a tournament be given here to which the knights of France, aye, even the knights of England and Spain, be bidden to show their skill—yet even then shall these of your following triumph in the lists and great shall be the glory of the men of Alamayne!"

The Emperor thought upon these words of Duke Raoul

and to him also it did appear a pleasant and notable plan, and straightway he did agree that this would be so. And he caused to be sent out to the four ways of the world heralds and trumpeters to proclaim the giving of such a tournament to be held at his city of Mayence within the half year.

But Raoul smiled secretly to himself and, when again among those of his own household, being full merry with the wine he had drunk that night, he gave open voice to the dark plotting he had done, so that divers of his lords heard him say:

"This Huon of Bordeaux has been widely bespoken as a man of war, full of cunning and high deeds. Such a man will not remain aloof from the Emperor's tournament. And he is hardly more than a green youth in years, while I have spent many seasons in the field. Thus when I shall challenge him to single combat let no man fear the ending. Huon shall die beneath my sword and his lands and lady will drop into my hands as easily as the ripe fruit falls from its parent tree in the proper season."

Among those lords who listened to this unworthy boasting was one Godrun of Noremberg who in his boyhood had served as a page in the household of Duke Sevin of Bordeaux. And many had been the kindnesses shown him there. Also he had sported with Huon when they had both been lads scarce out of childhood and together they had learned to swing swords and hold lances, giving many a stout blow to each other during that learning. So that Godrun now looked upon Duke Raoul with much disfavor and determined in his heart that this fell plan would be spoiled if he could have the doing of it.

He called his squire and together they slipped away from the Emperor's court and rode with all speed into France and even into the city of Bordeaux with little rest or food and drink to sustain them.

Now Huon had encompassed the keep held in defiance by Angelars and, although those within fought bravely and with much spirit, yet were they in the end defeated and the keep taken. Then did Huon hang the traitor Angelars upon his own high tower and with him divers of his captains.

But he freed those of the common sort who had but served their lord in this bad business. Having done so he returned to Bordeaux, meeting on the way those heralds who had been sent out by the Emperor to summon all the knights of Christendom to the tournament at Mayence. And hearing of this Huon and his men were much pleased and decided to go thither at the proper time to win honor and glory for the realm of France.

The Duchess Claramonde knew great joy and happiness when her lord returned thus speedily to her without hurt and she caused a feast to be made so that all might partake and so share in her pleasure. To this feast came Godrun of Noremberg, all unknowing, with his distressful knowledge of the plot against his friend. He contrived to have speech privately with Duke Huon and his lady.

"Lord Duke, in former years when your father, the mighty Sevin, still walked this earth, I dwelt happily in these halls as one of his fosterlings. You I did know well then and ofttimes we did strive together in sport. Now it is with shame and sorrow that I come into your presence with such a story on my lips.

"For know you this—now am I liege man to that Duke Raoul who is nephew to the Emperor of Alamayne. And this Raoul is a mighty lord in battle, none of the knights of Christendom has been able to stand against him lance to lance, sword to sword, shield to shield, and come the better from the encounter. But in other ways he is not so great a man.

"Hearing tales of the beauty and courtesy of this lady, your Duchess, he put on him the sorry guise of a pilgrim and came even into this very hall. Beholding the lady, he coveted her to be his wife and is determined to make his wishes in this matter true. You he holds of little account because of your youth and because Bordeaux is not as large as the fief he rules. So he has caused his uncle, the Emperor, to proclaim a tournament to draw you to Mayence where he may challenge you to single combat and kill you, taking both your lady and your land unto himself!"

Now, upon hearing this, the heart of Huon did swell

with red rage that such an insult should be laid upon his lady and upon him. And he drew out his sword so that the torchlight in the hall did fall full upon his blade as he cried:

"Should this black-hearted Duke have · a hundred full armed knights in his train and I stand alone but for this blade, yet will I face him in battle!"

And the Duchess Claramonde rose in her place, her eyes, too, full of the fire of war. And she said:

"Husband, right well do you speak! This Raoul is no true knight, nay, by his action he denies the very sword and spurs he wears. So hot am I against him that I would I might put on coat-mail and helm and ride at your right hand in such array when you go up against him!"

Huon laughed right joyfully at her words and said to Godrun:

"You see, friend, this is our temper and it shall be the undoing of so proud and willful a lord as this Duke Raoul. I have heard at all times good report of your Emperor who men bespeak as a just and generous lord. Now I shall ride to him and ask for his word upon the matter."

Thus it was decided and, with Godrun and others who were of his following, Huon set forth for the city of Mayence.

III. HOW HUON SETTLED HIS QUARREL WITH RAOUL, TRUSTING IN THE EMPEROR'S JUSTICE

BUT WHILE THEY yet were some distance from Mayence, Huon summoned to him his principal knights and made plain to them his desire—that he ride alone to the court of the Emperor, since this quarrel with Duke Raoul was his only and not to be pursued by other men. All raised their voices and spoke against him in this matter, but he would not be gainsaid and, in the end, it went as he willed and he rode alone into the stronghold of the enemy.

Now the Emperor had decreed feasting for all comers and welcomed to his own table those knights who were minded to try their fortune at the jousting. When Huon came into the city, all clad in mail, his helm on his head, lance in hand, he rode straight into the hall of the Emperor where all the court sat in merriment and good cheer over their meat. And all there were greatly amazed to see a knight in such warlike guise ride in amongst them. So that the Emperor called thus to him with his own voice:

"Ha, sir knight, and what manner of man be you to ride so boldly and in such rude, warlike dress into this company? Know you not that I be Emperor of all this land and to me men do full courtesy?"

At the right hand of the Emperor sat the Duke Raoul. No armor was on him, no helm hid his comely face. But he was clad in a seemly robe of rich crimson with much gold thread worked into it in a cunning manner, showing a hunt with hounds and hart in full cry. Though his heart was foul yet his appearance was fair, and of all the lords there assembled at that time he was the best to look upon—saving only Huon.

But when the Duke of Bordeaux did gaze upon the face of his enemy and thought of all which had been reported to him by Godrun concerning Raoul, he did believe the Emperor's nephew like unto a demon out of Hell. And his rage arose in his throat until it was like to choke him, so that he needs must turn aside his eyes from Raoul lest he be moved by his hate to strike him down where he sat in such ease and splendor.

So Huon came before the Emperor and made answer to him clearly.

"Lord Emperor, I am liege man to Charlemagne of France and have come hither to try my fortune in the tournament which your heralds have proclaimed throughout Christendom. But in this hour I stand here before you for another cause, also, for I would ask of you justice—since you are renowned for your fair dealing with all men."

And the Emperor smiled upon Huon and he put forth his hand to urge silence upon all those who sat there.

"Never hath any man, gentle or common, come crying to me for justice that I did not make full answer according to the wits and heart the good God granted to me at my birthing. Speak on, stranger, what is your plaint?"

And Huon straightway told his story.

"This is how it has fared with me, Lord Emperor. Know you that I hold a fief of some small wealth, which I am lord of by right of birth and the might of my sword arm. And also, by the Grace of the Lord Jesu, I rejoice in the love of a fair lady whom I won to wife after many fell dangers and much bitter suffering.

"When I was from home on affairs of my fief, a lord of your following did come in disguise into my keep for no other purpose than to look upon my lady of whom he had heard much report. When he saw her he did purpose to take her for his own, deeming me of little account and not to be held in esteem. Yea, he even made sport of me before his men, saying that he would easily slay me in this tournament and take my wife and my fief for his own.

"So do I ride to you in the guise of war, that I may demand justice against this villain. Now do I cast down my glove and face him sword to sword and shield to shield that I may wrack upon his body the punishment he deserves!"

But black now was the Emperor's face and hot his voice as he made answer:

"Such a man is not worthy to be called in combat, as if he were truly a belted knight of honor and goodly life. Therefore, if it be true that he is man of mine, I give you full leave to slay him wherever you may chance upon him and in whatever degree he now abides!"

Upon hearing these words of the Emperor, Huon slipped from the saddle of his horse, putting aside the lance he had borne into the hall. And he drew forth from its scabbard his sword. Taking a quick step to the high table, he raised the visor of his helm so that those there might look upon his face. And then he cried out to Duke Raoul:

"Traitor, false and perjured knight! Look upon that Huon of Bordeaux whom you did plot to send to his death. Bordeaux and my Lady Claramonde are not for you!"

Then raising his sword he did run it through the body of Raoul, slaying him before he could rise out of his seat.

Whereupon all those who abode in the hall gave forth cries of fear and anger. And principal among these was the Emperor, who called upon his guards to cut down this murderer.

But Huon turned then upon the Emperor, crying:

"So this be your true practice, Lord Emperor? That since it is a kinsman of yours who is the offender, justice shall not be done. If your justice turns so easily, I want none of it. This shall uphold my case against yours!"

He leaped into the saddle and held aloft his sword still all bedrabbled with the blood of Raoul. Then he went up against those of the guard who tried to stay him and he cut his way through them, fighting as one of the great heroes of old. And many men did he wound and slay before he won free out of the city of Mayence.

By the Emperor's order all those knights who rode under the banners of Alamayne got to horse and pursued Huon across the plain. And with them rode the Emperor himself, mounted on his charger Amphage—mate to which there was none in the whole world. So great was the rage of the Emperor that he spurred out before his men and so came close to Huon.

Huon, seeing this, stayed his flight a little and waited upon the Emperor. And they came together with such force that the Emperor was thrown from the back of Amphage and his leg was broken in twain. Then did Huon look upon his enemy with pity in his heart, and he raised no sword against him. Instead he left his tired horse and, mounted upon Amphage, rode away. And the Emperor was taken up by those who followed him.

But because Huon did pity his enemy and leave him living on the field, much sorrow and bitterness were to be his portion.

IV. HOW THE EMPEROR BROUGHT WAR TO BORDEAUX AND THAT CITY WAS REDUCED TO SORE STRAIT

HUON CAME INTO the encampment of those who had followed him from Bordeaux and he straightway set before them how ill his mission had fared. So they arrayed themselves for the battle which was speedily brought upon them when the knights and lords of Alamayne, hot with anger, came at a full gallop. But the knights and men of Bordeaux were no green youths entering into their first assay of arms untried. And they were led by Huon and by the crafty Gerames who had grown old in warfare.

So did those of Bordeaux fashion a wall of steel which held fast against the enemies' charge. And full many of the Emperor's men were struck from their saddles to their death beneath the iron shod hooves of their own chargers. Huon fought not like one man but as twenty. From one end of the field to the other his sword cleared him an open path and naught was behind him but men newly dead.

Thus at last the Emperor, who had been watching from a litter the manner of this desperate affray, began to bemoan the slaughter of his men, for it was like to be that none of them might survive the field. At the same time Gerames spurred to ride stirrup to stirrup with Huon and say:

"Lord Duke, we have made much grievous slaughter among these proud men of Alamayne. The Emperor himself has been laid low by your own skill and courage. But after the way of battles, we have lost divers good knights and sturdy bow and pike men, too. This be the land of Alamayne and the Emperor can call to him fresh men. But Bordeaux lies many leagues away and how can we summon any to fill the gaps which death has holed in our battle line?"

Huon, thinking upon this, believed that Gerames spoke with his usual wisdom and he answered:

"Let us send a herald unto the Emperor and ask if he will make truce. Then shall we withdraw into our own land where the advantage will be ours. Send forth a herald of your choosing with trumpeters, and have him seek out the leader of the men of Alamayne thus—"

And so was it done. In spite of the Emperor's great and abiding hate for Huon, he needs must agree to the truce, thinking to himself the while that when his leg was healed and he could call up fresh liege men he would pursue the Duke of Bordeaux even to the walls of his own city and that he would rive that same city with fire and sword and reduce it to naught in the eyes of all men. But for that he must bide his time. So did he agree to a six months' truce to hold betwixt them.

Thereafter the armies parted from each other, both licking their wounds—even as a lion and a tiger evenly matched might agree to fight no more, but retreat into their private dens to hoard their strength against another meeting.

Huon came back to Bordeaux with the greatest speed possible and he related to the Lady Claramonde how he had served Duke Raoul and what had come from his vengeance. The Lady Claramonde, greatly fearing of the future, said unto her lord:

"Husband, this Emperor ruleth all the reaches of Alamayne which, it has been said, is even greater than France. He can call to his banner a hundred knights for every man who owes you field service. Mayhap he can crack Bordeaux like a nut between his two fingers. Emperor Charlemagne is lately dead and in his stead ruleth the child Louis. He hates you for the sake of his dead brother whom you slew by chance, and he will not come hither to aid you with as much as one arrow!"

"True," Huon made her sober answer. "Therefore we of Bordeaux must trust in the grace and goodness of Our Lord Jesu and do the best that we can against the coming of a dark future."

"France may not aid us but there is help beyond our borders if we will seek it, my lord. In Tunis is my brother, now the Dey and overlord, and he has a thousand times

a thousand men to rally to his battle cry. Think not that he is
an unbeliever, for long since did he accept Our Lord Jesu
for his own and is a Christian man. In our childhood there
was strong love between us twain and I do not think that I
am yet wholly forgotten by him. Do you then take ship,
husband, and get you overseas to Tunis. There call upon my
brother and return with the army he will freely give into
your service. So you can meet the Emperor with an equal
force!"

But Huon frowned and made dissenting answer:

"Wife, if I slip away now from Bordeaux and sail overseas
to secure this aid you speak of, I shall then be deserting
those who trust in me, and they may freely name me coward
and false knight. Much may chance on such a voyage and I
may not return therefrom, leaving my city to a black fate.
Nay, here I must stay and share what may come."

So did he answer all the pleas of Claramonde. And her
fear of the future did press upon her heart as if a rock had
settled therein.

All the defenses of Bordeaux were made stronger, and
food and drink were brought into the city, the carts moving
through all gates from sunrise to sunset. Out in the land
Gerames had put many watchers and swift messengers to
spy upon the coming of the men of Alamayne and all
within the city worked with a will to be ready.

At last came the word that the banners of Alamayne
were to be seen on the borders of the duchy and that the
forces of the Emperor were laying waste—burning and slaying as they came. Then did the men of Huon's following
withdraw within the stout walls of the city. A store of arrows
and crossbow bolts were brought up, swords and lances
were made ready and they waited.

Soon enough the forces of Alamayne came before the city
and set up a camp of many tents. That night their campfires
made a blazing ring without end, encircling the walls of
Bordeaux.

Then did Huon say to Gerames:

"Look you how this Emperor takes his ease before my
walls, setting out his meat and drink to consume at leisure

because he thinks us entrapped, to be taken and slain whene'er he wishes. Let us issue forth and show him what manner of prey he seeks!"

So did a picked force come silently out of the city by a postern gate and they rode as swift as the wind, silent as the clouds of the night, down upon the enemy camp. There they wrought such damage as the Alamayne force did think might be done by demons. Full many knights died that hour, and the Emperor was fain to cry aloud with rage and pain.

But Huon's force withdrew into the city again, with joy and ease of heart because of the grievous blow that they had successfully dealt. And the Duke said to his men:

"Where is Sir Gerames? I do not hear his voice raised in our rejoicing."

Then a knight, wounded almost unto death, rode forward crying:

"Alas, Lord Duke, in that last charge Sir Gerames was swept from his horse and if he be not dead, then he is surely in the hands of the enemy!"

V. HOW GERAMES WAS BROUGHT OUT OF MORTAL DANGER AND HUON WAS FORCED TO SEEK AID

GERAMES, BLEEDING from many wounds and helpless, was brought before the Emperor, who was overjoyed at the capture of a lord so high in the council of the enemy. And in high good humor he called forth to the men of his host:

"Here have we one of these stout villains who oppose us. Now, to the man who brings me Huon also so humbled, will I give both this proud city of Bordeaux and the Lady Claramonde herself."

But Gerames faced him right proudly and with head held high, saying in return:

"Bold words, my Lord Emperor, bold words. Not yet have you or any man of yours won within the gates of Bordeaux save that he went so as a prisoner of ours. And

Duke Huon shall hold those same gates fast against all comers as long as it be needful. No knight in all the land of Alamayne can take this city or humble its lord!"

And at this speech from a captive, standing chained and unarmed, the Emperor was wroth indeed, and he turned to his marshal, Sir Otho, ordering him in this wise:

"Take forth this graybearded fool and any we have captured with him, build high a gallows nigh unto the city wall. And when that be finished—hang them all!"

Sir Otho stirred not from his place, but rather cautioned his liege lord with these words:

"Sire, if we do your will in this matter then shall those of Bordeaux be moved to act likewise against men of ours who lie captive behind their walls. Pray you, by the grace of Our Lord Jesu, think again before you order this thing."

But the Emperor turned upon him a face so black with wrath that he needs must obey. And sorrowfully he led forth Gerames and divers other men of Bordeaux who had been taken in the battle.

By the walls of Bordeaux, hardly a bowshot length beyond the main gate, the men of Alamayne erected a wide gallows. And those within the city came to stand upon the battlements and look down to see what was being done. Huon beat his fists upon the harsh stone and called forth:

"Shall we allow our brothers-in-arms to be so served? Let all who will helm and horse and follow me. For if we allow this to be done to them then shall never again our honor be bright in the sight of men!"

And all those who could sit horse or draw a bow made ready to issue out in rescue.

Once again Sir Otho had gone in to the Emperor and there, holding himself humbly, made again a plea for mercy.

"Sire, truly has this Duke Huon hurt your heart when he slew before your eyes the Duke Raoul whom you loved right well. But let him pay for this in Christian wise. Let him voyage to the Holy Land and there do proper penance. Do you send now a herald unto the city and—"

But no more words left his lips for the Emperor gave a roar of rage—like unto the roar of a wounded boar—and Sir

Otho was forced away by his friends lest the Emperor order him hanged also. Sadly the marshal returned to the foot of the gallows. But there he set no guard and he delayed the hanging as long as he might, hoping that the Emperor might yet relent his harshness.

There came a brazen clang as down fell the drawbridge of Bordeaux and out of that city came a desperate band of fighting men. Down upon the gallows they whirled and there they cut free the prisoners, while another force spurred ahead to use sword and lance upon the men of Alamayne. Before the Emperor could order his army, they were back again into the city—only with them they had swept Sir Otho and a hundred more of the enemy.

These Huon would have used even as the Emperor had ordered done to the men of Bordeaux—hanging them together from the battlements. But Gerames spoke for them, telling all that Sir Otho had done to make peace. So Huon pardoned the prisoners in the name of his beloved friend.

Now that very night there was born to Duke Huon and the Lady Claramonde a daughter. And about her cradle in the keep there appeared divers of the ladies of Elfland, each bringing to the child her blessing and the promise that she would wear a crown and rule as a powerful and well-beloved queen. But the chief of these ladies looked most sorrowfully upon Huon and his duchess and she spoke through falling tears:

"Lord Duke and Lady Duchess, sore are our hearts in Elfland and we grieve for you and for this fair Clarette, born your daughter. By the Law of Fairies King Oberon cannot succor you in this distress since he had proclaimed that after him you shall reign our king and queen and to that estate you must now win by your own strength and endeavor. He bids me tell you that you shall not again look upon his face until that distant hour when you twain will meet for the last time. So wait no longer to seek for aid—if you have any to seek!"

When the Elf ladies had gone Huon called to him his herald, Herbourny, and instructed him in this wise:

"Raise you the flag of truce and ride into the camp of the

Alamayne men. There seek out the Emperor and say to him that much blood has been spent by both of us in this quarrel. But if he will declare an end to warfare, then shall I make submission unto him as a vassal to his rightful lord, holding Bordeaux by his permission—since the King of France has come not to my aid. And likewise I shall go to the Sepulcher of Our Lord Jesu in the Holy Land to pray for the good of all of us. But if the Emperor says nay to this, then shall we fight on until the last stone be tumbled from our walls!"

So did Herbourny bear the message given him by Huon, and the lords of Alamayne would have been content with the terms the Duke proposed. But the Emperor, mad with hate, would have none of it and drove the herald from him with threats.

Huon then summoned to him all the principal men of Bordeaux. And when they were assembled within the hall of the keep, he told them of the failure of his attempt to make terms. Then he added:

"Men of Bordeaux, we have but little meat or drink left within our walls. In each sally good knights and men go to their deaths so in time there will be none of us left to hold sword against the enemy. Louis of France will send us no aid.

"But Salybrant, brother to my lady, rules as Dey in Tunis. He is a Christian man and may aid us for the love he bears the Duchess. Thus our only hope remains that I go forth secretly from this city and seek him out to beg help. Be this your will also?"

And all assembled there, knowing how dark was the future, agreed that he must do this thing. So he set Gerames in his place as leader of the men of Bordeaux. Then having taken leave of his lady and their daughter he slipped away in the night with only a few followers.

VI. HOW IT FARED WITH THOSE WHO HELD BORDEAUX AGAINST THE WRATH OF THE EMPEROR

MANY AND VALOROUS were the deeds of the men of Bordeaux holding their city against the enemy. But in every charge from out its gates, and in every fight upon the walls, men fell under the bite of the sword or by the swift shaft of the arrow. And none arose from out of the dust to take their places. So that fewer and fewer were able to answer the call to arms of the battle trumpets.

And Gerames, seeing every hour his lines grow thinner, his men fall to return no more, sorrowed in his heart. But with all he kept a brisk tongue and a bright face for the Lady Claramonde. While she, donning heavy mail over her tender flesh, did walk the walls and draw a bow of her own, sending full many straightly aimed arrows into the Alamayne camp.

But at length came a dark day when the mayor of the city waited upon the Duchess to say unto her:

"Liege lady, within this city are many stout hearts and strong arms to your service. But food and drink are needed by all men. Wide now stands the granary door and naught lies within the bins there but the dust of the wheat which once filled them. We have not tasted meat this fortnight past and ill seems the future."

Then up spake Gerames in answer:

"True, fighting men must eat and we cannot hold the walls save when we have the proper strength to do so. In the fields beyond the river there graze cattle and sheep brought hither by our enemy for his service. This night let us issue forth and sweep them up!"

So was it decided in a council of war and Gerames, with the best of the fighters still living, came secretly out into the fields. But the Emperor's man on watch there was no dullard and he gave the alarm so swiftly that Gerames' men were struck while yet they were gathering the cattle together. And in the dark was fought a grim battle.

Ill indeed was the fortune of the men of Bordeaux. Some were swept into the river where, weighted down by their mail, they went to death in the waters, none hearing their cries for help. And others fell under the sword and lance or, lying wounded in the press, were trampled by the horses. Thus died the last of the strong fighting men of Bordeaux.

And among them was Gerames, who had been slave to the Saracens, hermit in the desert lands, and a good friend to Huon all his days. Bravely he died as became a belted knight, slain by honorable wounds as a warrior of fame. And with him died the hope and deliverance of the Lady Claramonde and her daughter.

Bernard, who had been squire to Gerames, won free after the fall of his master and fought his way by sheer strength of his body to the gates of the city. There he did spur to the keep where, all blood and dust from the field, he ran through the halls seeking out the duchess.

The Lady Claramonde, seeing him in such sore straits, did guess somewhat of his dire news before he gave it tongue.

But when he cried: "On the field lies even now my master, the noble Gerames—" she gave such a scream as might one faced by doom, and then she stood statue still until those about her thought her mind gone from reason of the blow. But in time she turned to them and, when she spoke, it was evenly and with a calm voice.

"With Gerames, who was our fortress and our shield, reft from us, we cannot hope to prevail against the Emperor who can call to his service full half of Europe, while we have not enough left to man the walls. Too late will my lord return with the help he has gone to seek. But be sure, friends, that when again he rides in France it will be to avenge this hour and us. Now I will go up into the gate and from the window there I shall hail this Emperor and see what terms he will grant us in his triumph. But first, Bernard, I would speak with you."

She took the squire into the fair part of the hall where they were alone and there she did give him certain orders,

namely that he was to go to the stable and there saddle
with his own hands the horse Amphage which Huon had
won from the Emperor in battle. Then she would send to
him secretly one of her maidens with the child Clarette.
And the baby he was to bear to Cluny and there give her
into the safe keeping of the Abbot, who was uncle to Huon
and his good friend.

"For," said the Lady Claramonde, "the Emperor may take
Bordeaux by reason of our weakness and me he may make
prisoner. But this child who be heir to Huon shall be saved
from his wrath.

And Bernard swore by the Cross that he would guard the
child even to his heart's blood and bear her safely to the
Abbey of Cluny. Then he made haste to the stable and had
forth Amphage, the horse being fresh and eager for the road.
Hardly had he made secure the saddle upon the charger's
back than down came the maid, slipping through the shadows bearing in her arms—close wrapped in a dark cloak—
the little Clarette. And with the babe before him the squire
made his way out of Bordeaux by a little known way and
reached the fields beyond the town. Once free he put
spurs to Amphage and rode at a gallop into the night
toward Cluny.

When the maid reported to the Lady Claramonde that
her daughter was in Bernard's keeping and that the squire
had set forth, the Duchess went up into the gate and caused
torches to be set up there so that those without the gate
might see her standing so. And then she ordered her trum-
peter to sound parley.

This being reported to the Emperor, he came himself on
horseback, and, looking up at the lady standing framed by
torchlight, he thought her very young and fair and he knew
pity for her. But remembering that she was wife to Huon
he hardened his heart and waited in silence to hear what
she had to say.

"Lord Emperor"—loud and clear, without tears or breaking, sounded the voice of the Lady Claramonde—"defense-
less against your might lies this city of Bordeaux at this
hour, since you have broken our strength at last and put

to lance and sword our men. But you and those who follow you be Christian men and as Christians I ask that you deal with us mercifully as Our Lord Jesu has taught."

"Lady," replied the Emperor, "be assured that this city shall not be put to sack if you now surrender yourselves to me. And I promise to deal with you and yours after no barbaric manner."

With that half promise she needs must be content. But in her heart she was glad that she had sent forth her daughter while there was yet time.

So was Bordeaux surrendered and the Emperor did not sack it but set over it his own governor. And those who had been men of Huon and were still living he took with him to Mayence. There were they set in prison and the Lady Claramonde was placed in a stout tower where she did not even see the face of her keeper. And her heart was nigh to breaking when she thought upon her evil plight, her only hope lying in the swift return of Huon.

VII. OF HUON'S VOYAGE THROUGH STORMY SEAS AND HIS COMING TO THE CASTLE ADAMANT

HUON AND THOSE with him, having stolen away through the forces of the enemy, came at length to a port of the sea. And there the Duke made inquiries concerning a ship to take him and his companions unto Tunis. But it was the season of wild storms in the outer ocean, and few captains desired to risk their craft to the tearing winds and raging waters. But, after many days, Huon found a sailing master willing to try his fortune, and so they set sail.

Just beyond the protection of the harbor their vessel was caught up by the wind and fled helpless before a storm through seas which were mountains of foam and water. No man amongst them, no matter what his knowledge, could control their flight, and they knew not whither they sailed. Within the ship they were flung hither and thither so that all were sore bruised and Huon did strain his sword arm so that he could not raise it from his side. Thus did they exist for several days, and in all that time they sighted not the sun nor knew if it were day or night which encompassed them.

Then there appeared across the sky before them a band of sullen fire and there was a sound to be heard even above the fury of the wind, a sound like unto the crackling of flames. The master of the ship, weak and trembling so that he could hardly stand upon his two feet, came to Huon and said:

"My Lord Duke, now we poor sinners be indeed undone and utterly lost, for the storm has driven us over the edge of the world and before us now lie the iron gates of Hell— even as legend has reported it!"

Huon looked upon that band of flames and listened to that dolorous moaning which seemed to issue therefrom, and he, too, knew fear. But he stood straight and faced to it, saying:

"We be but mortal men and so full of sin. But on this sailing we come with clean hearts and the wish to aid those weaker than ourselves. So by the promises made us by Lord Jesu, I say to you now—fear not. For Hell shall not engulf us, nor swallow us this day!"

And he spoke the truth, for though the current of the waters bore them close to those iron gates which bar that foul place and they heard the wailing of the lost within, yet did they escape Hell and were carried on. At length the flames faded from the sky and before them they saw a point of honest sunlight piercing through the gloom.

This beam struck full upon a rocky mountain rising out of the sea, a mountain as black as the stormy night which lay behind them. But on its crown was a castle of purest white so that Huon and all those within the ship took heart with looking upon it, for it must be the keep of some great lord who would give them rest and shelter.

Straight toward the mountain of rock drove the vessel, and now the master again looked wan and afraid as he cried aloud:

"Alas! We are the most unfortunate of men! This be the

castle and the rock of Adamant, which is truly a trap to catch honest sailors. Know you that there is that in this rock which draws to it all of iron, even to the nails in the ship, and once it holds it never lets go again. They who come to Adamant go not forth from there again!"

From their ship they could now see about the foot of the mountain many other vessels, some old and rotted with time until they were crumbling into the water they rested upon. And into the heart of this dead fleet was drawn their own ship, pounding to bits many of the wrecks about it.

But as the day faded it appeared to Huon that lights shone out in the windows of the castle above and he wished to climb the rock and seek help, since the store of food and water they had on board was but a small one. But still was his arm useless to him, so that he himself could not attempt such a feat.

Then did one of his men, Sir Arnold, who came from mountain country and had ofttimes climbed among rocks for sport, stand out and say that he would assay the climb. And he put aside his mail and all weapons but his belt knife. They wished him well as he began to scramble across the slimy rock near the sea where the spray dashed high.

The way to the castle was not too difficult and he came at length to the main gate. There he paused and hailed those who might be within. But no one answered him save the rising wind, nor could he see any sentry on the battlements or hear anything move within.

Since the gate stood ajar he ventured inside. But there was no man or woman to be seen in all the courtyard. It was like a house of the long since dead. As he lingered there, shivering a little with cold and loneliness, he heard at last a sound, but not that of honest footsteps. And he turned to see gliding across the pavement a loathly serpent. Taller than the wall behind, it reared its fanged head and from its open jaws dripped green venom to spatter on the stones.

Sir Arnold, having naught but his belt knife to defend himself, fled for his life, dodging the serpent and winning down the rock again to the ship. There he told what he had seen, saying that death, fanged and scaled, crawled through those halls above and no mortal man might go safely there.

So did those on the ship know despair, for their food grew less with each passing day and men dropped in their weakness and could not keep their feet. But a second ship drove in among the pack of wrecks and this was manned by pirates. Huon called upon his men to arm and fight and they did take the pirate ship and put those within to the sword. For a while thereafter they had the provisions found there to stay them and they knew hope again.

But in no way could they free their vessel from the grip of Adamant and as the weeks passed one by one they sickened and died, some from starvation, some from illness bred by the rotten ships about them, and some from lack of hope. Only Huon would not allow his heart to faint for he kept ever before him the thought of Bordeaux and those who lay behind its walls trusting in him. And he swore that he would do all in the power of mortal man in their behalf.

Then came the morning when he was the only living man to rise from his couch, all alone on the ship. And nowhere was there a mouthful of bread or water to assuage his hunger and thirst. He knew that death was very nigh to him. But he determined that if that be so it would be a death of his own choosing. And, though his body was weak so that he had to rest many times, he donned his mail and helm and belted on his sword.

Then he turned to the rock and called out in a loud and ringing voice:

"Monster or demon, I, Huon of Bordeaux, do come now and I bring your death upon the point of my steel."

Then he began to ascend the rock, having to go slowly because of his great weakness and the pain which still made his sword arm heavy. But after a time he came out upon the top of the mountain and saw before him the gates of the castle. The sun touched to golden fire certain words graven on these gates which Huon read, this being the warning of Adamant.

"Let him who enters herein beware, for unless he be the worthiest of mortal knights with a body like unto steel,

88

this venture shall prove his last. But if his courage fails not—then let him enter."

And Huon, drawing his sword, entered into the castle of Adamant.

VIII. OF THE CASTLE ADAMANT AND ITS LOATHLY GUARDIAN

IN THE COURTYARD there was nothing living to be seen—not even a bird—and a deep silence hung over the place, which Huon thought must be like unto the silence which abides within a tomb. In him his heart grew chill and he knew the coldness of true fear.

Then out of the silence there came a sound, a strange slithering noise which was not made, he knew, by mortal man. And he saw, coming forth from the inner hall, the loathly serpent which Sir Arnold had spoken of.

Many spans high swung its head and its blazing eyes were like unto flaming lamps. In its mouth its tongue flickered back and forth like the lash of a slaver's whip and its fangs dripped green and acid venom. These fangs were as long as a stout man's arm and there seemed to be no end to the scaled body of the creature.

When it saw Huon it hissed and screamed and coiled across the pavement. Huon held his shield before him and stood ready with his sword. But the monster lunged a blow with its blunt head and, catching the edge of the shield with one of its fangs, tore the iron apart as if it were but rotted wood.

Huon's sword struck straight and true upon its body but the scales there were as the stoutest armor and the steel blade slipped down without cutting through them.

Again the serpent drew back its head for a fatal stroke. And now Huon flung from him the riven shield and useless sword, knowing the darkness of despair. Then he chanced to sight a lance leaning against the inner gate, a lance shining

and barbed and longer than any he had ever seen before. This he seized upon before the serpent struck.

Holding it fast in his two hands he braced the butt on the stones of the courtyard pavement, steadying it with all the strength in his body. And when the serpent's head loomed above him he moved so that the lance pierced up into its mouth and through that into its brain. Thus did it die with many writhings and coilings of its loathsome body.

Faint and weak Huon stumbled on into the hall of the castle and there did he halt amazed at what he saw. For not even the court of the Emperor could boast such richness.

There were five and twenty great pillars and some of these were of a marble as purely white as the walls of Heaven, and some of a marble as dark as night, and some of jasper and some of sardonyx. And about the walls and entwined upon these pillars was a vine of soft gold, wrought with marvelous subtlety so that it seemed a living thing. And hanging from this vine were clusters of grapes, but they were formed of amethyst and emeralds and rubies, more than might be contained in the ranson of a hundred kings. Light shone from these stones, making bright all that long hall.

The flooring whereon he trod was a mosaic patterned with the deeds of heroes, but heroes he knew not. And beyond this hall were divers other chambers all rich and of a surpassing beauty, with baths of gleaming crystal, containing likewise coffers and chests full of all manner of clothing such as the greatest lords of the earth might be proud to wear.

Then did Huon put off his armor and lave his body in a cooling bath. And he donned a fine robe of soft blue and set about his loins a belt of sapphire and gold. Thus apparelled, he further explored the castle and found at last a walled garden wherein grew ripe fruit. And on this did he break his fast, though still he longed for meat and bread.

That night he slept in an ivory bed, full weary from all which had happened to him. But in the morning he awoke refreshed. And having eaten again of the fruit, he wandered anew through Adamant. So did he learn that there was no road out of this wondrous castle save back down the rock to the dead ships. And he feared that he must spend his days there a prisoner for life.

Despairing, he sank down upon a thronelike seat fashioned of beaten gold which stood in a little room all to itself. And casting his eyes to the floor because of his sorrow, he chanced to see certain words set there in the paving.

"O, man of courage," he read, "if you be also free of sin, take then the key which lies to your hand and use it here."

And below these words he saw a keyhole of gold, while on the arm of the throne there was chained a key. Kneeling he set this into the lock and turned. There came the sound of stones moving in their beds and that portion of the pavement on which lay the writing tilted up, showing beneath it a stair. Down these steps went Huon, for he deemed that his case could be no worse than now it was.

Below he found a long vaulted hallway wherein was set an oven of stone. And two men served this oven, bringing out fair loaves of bread and setting dough in their place. They worked in silence, nor did they make an answer when Huon asked them whence they came or who they were. Angered at last he set himself in the path of one and seized tight upon the sleeve of his tunic.

Then the man turned upon him, frowning, and said:

"Rash mortal, why do you so disturb my labor?" And he tried to pull free his sleeve from Huon's grip. But the Duke would not let him go.

"In the Name of Our Lord Jesu and those who dwell in Heaven, I beg you give me to eat of your bread, for I have been fasting for these many days—"

The servingman still frowned, but he answered quickly:

"If you be Christian man and without sin, then you may eat freely of our viands. Go you to the table yonder and break your fast as you will. But know you—our food be death to those who eat treacherously of it. This is a fairy castle and we are bound here to serve in silence for a thousand years. Nor shall we speak to you again!"

Then he twitched his sleeve from out Huon's fingers and

went back to his work. Nor would he answer any question Huon asked of him thereafter.

So Huon went to the table at the far side of the room and there he discovered all manner of meat and drink laid out upon it. And he feasted as he had not since he left Bordeaux. Thus passed many days in the Castle of Adamant. And every day Huon tried to find a way out of that place, but there was none.

Then one night there came a storm which appeared like to tear the castle from its roots on the rock. And when he went forth in the morning and looked down upon the place of ships he saw that many had been pounded into bits against the rock by the waves.

But even as he watched a new vessel appeared on the edge of the sea and was borne toward Adamant by that fatal enchantment which made the mountain a trap. Huon sorrowed to see the coming of more companions in misfortune. But he climbed down the mountain to lend aid to any who might win to shore.

IX. OF THE COMING OF THE GRIFFIN AND HUON'S ESCAPE FROM ADAMANT

THOSE UPON THE ship in the bay gave thanks upon reaching land in safety. Now half of them were Saracen and half Christian men who had been taken up by the mariners from a barren rock after a storm had shattered their vessel. When they saw Huon all cried out to him for food, being sore distressed, for they had been driven before the winds for many days and what provisions they had carried were all gone.

So did Huon bring to them the bread and meat which were provided by the fairy men within the castle. But he cautioned them that only those who were Christian and of good heart could eat thereof without hurt. So did the Christians among the company take up the food and eat it and feel no ill. But the captain of the Saracens said unto Huon:

"Faint are we from hunger and nigh unto death. Yet a man who will betray his faith for meat in his belly is a false coward. Therefore we shall not eat."

But not all of his men were of the same mind and some gave over their belief and swore that they were Christian for the sake of food. But when they took into their mouths the bread from the castle it was as if they chewed upon a strong poison, and their hearts failed them and they died. Looking upon their bodies the Saracen captain laughed bitterly and spoke his thoughts aloud.

"The truth was not in them and so they died. The truth is in us but we shall also die, since we will not turn our coats for bread."

But Huon saluted him as one brave man to another, being true to himself and his belief. And the Duke climbed again the mountain and gathered the fruit of the walled garden. This he brought unto the Saracens so that they praised him much for the mercy and pity he had shown unto them.

Christians and Saracens together now entered Adamant with Huon and made free with all its treasures, abiding with good content within its walls. But Huon was still sore of mind and heart and wished to win free of that place—though he could see no manner of doing so.

Now it chanced that he came out upon the wall of the castle in the early morning. And so did he see a dark shadow which flashed across the sky, as there flew from the east a mighty griffin. So huge was this monster that its body darkened the rising sun and its wings spanned the walls of Adamant.

While Huon watched, the griffin dropped on closed wings to the splintered wreckage of the ships below and there it did choose one of the bodies of those Saracens who had died of their greed. In its talons it bore away the dead man, flying steadily off with its prey.

And seeing this Huon thought him of a plan, and he did determine to watch the following morning to see if the griffin would return or if its coming was but a chance happening.

So he arose with the dawn on the next day and went up on the battlements. Nor was he disappointed, for the griffin returned again and bore away one of the bodies.

Then Huon went down into the castle and brought forth his mail and his sword. Only shield he had none for the serpent had rent it apart with its fangs. And having made all ready, he told those who were in Adamant what he had chosen to do. All cried out against his plan, saying that his folly would only bring him to a horrible death, but he answered them firmly in this wise:

"There is no way out of Adamant for mortal man save this. And in Adamant I cannot bide happily nor at peace when I know that Bordeaux and all it contains, which is dearer to me than my life, lies in danger. So shall I attempt this way of escape by the aid of the griffin."

In the middle hour of the night, while it was still dark, he put on his mail and girt on his sword. So accoutered he climbed down the mountain to the wreckage and sought out the deck of the ship where lay the dead Saracens. And there he lay down among the dead and waited for the dawn.

With the light in the east came the griffin, its wings making thunder in the air. Huon lay unmoving, faint with hope. Down swooped the griffin and its claws fastened upon the Duke. But by reason of his mail they did not pierce his body. Up was he borne so fast that the wind rushed about him and he was fain to close his eyes upon a reeling heaven and earth.

The griffin flew steadily across the desert and cliffs surrounding Adamant until it came to a great rock standing like a pillar. On the crest of this was the nest where cried five offspring of the monster, their iron beaks gaping for the prey the mother bore. And into the midst of these did the parent griffin toss Huon.

Again his mail saved him from cruel death, for sharp as were the beaks and claws of the young griffins, they could not pierce to any vital spot of his body. And though they drew blood from his limbs he was not torn to pieces as they wished.

Escaping from their clutch, Huon drew his sword and did

battle with the young griffins, striking off the head of one, thrusting another through the heart, and at length slaying them all. But as he slew the last the parent monster returned and, seeing what had chanced with her fledglings, she screamed aloud her rage and struck down at Huon so that her beak cut deeply into his shoulder and he was like to be overborne and killed by the savageness of her attack.

Despairingly he thrust upward with his sword, and by good fortune cut through one of the griffin's legs, crippling the monster. Seeing that he had so gained the advantage, he aimed a second and third blow quickly and brought the creature to her death.

Worn and weak from his wounds he rested awhile and then, knowing that if he lingered there in that desert place he would die for want of food and water, he took up the great clawed foot of the griffin and climbed down from the nest rock.

In the far distance he could see the green of trees and he thought that there he might find water to ease his parched throat and lave his smarting wounds. He could travel but slowly for reason of his pain and distress, so that he was some hours crossing the hot, rocky land. And it was with weak and wavering feet that he came to a wide white gate and looked in upon a garden of such fairness that for a space he thought that he had truly died in that battle with the griffins and that now he had come to Paradise.

X. HOW HUON DID FEAST UPON THE APPLES OF PARADISE AND HEAR ILL NEWS OF BORDEAUX

COOL AND refreshing were the winds which blew across that garden and sweet they were with the scent of many flowers. So that when Huon came in, his feet making no sound upon the smooth greenness of the grass, he felt eased of his hurts of mind and body. Fruit of gold and of red and of purple hung heavy and ripe from trees and vines, and a multitude of birds sang through the hours of the day.

At length Huon came to a fountain of clear and crystal water which plumed high into the air and fell again into a basin curiously carved of pearl-tinted stone. Huon, looking upon this, was minded to rejoice in it and he freed himself from his wearying mail and leather and splashed into that pure flood.

Straightway, where the water laved his wounds, they healed leaving no scars to seam his flesh. And his weariness was gone so that he was as a strong man arising after a most refreshing sleep. Thus he lay for a time with his body within the embrace of the water of that fountain until all was well with him again.

Then, coming out of the flooded basin, he saw a tree set apart from the others of the grove, its boughs bending to the ground by reason of the fruit it bore in great quantity. And this fruit was as golden as the sun and from it came a delightful odor which drew him to it. He picked one and found that he held an apple, perfect in all its shape. Slowly he ate the fruit, and throughout his body it seemed that the blood did run more swiftly and his heart grow lighter, and he said aloud:

"How I would that my dear Claramonde stood here with me now and that she held in her arms our dear daughter, that we might be free of our miseries in this garden of Paradise. For certainly this be indeed that Paradise which sinful man so willfully lost!"

And, having finished the apple, he reached forth his hand to pluck a second.

But at that moment a bright column of light appeared beside the tree and within it stood a Being who seemed bodied in flame. So bright and of such fire was this figure that Huon was fain to cover his two eyes with his hands when he strove to look upon it. And the Being spoke aloud in a voice which was like the peal of silver-tongued bells.

"Huon, Duke of Bordeaux!"

Then did Huon fall upon his knees, and he dared not look

upon the exceeding brightness of the Being but answered in an humble voice:

"Aye, Lord?"

"Call me not 'lord,' Huon, for I am but the messenger of those who are greater than I. But list well now to what I have to say unto you, for sad and drear is the news I bear. Oh, Huon, stout must you steel your heart against the hearing of it now.

"Know you that your city of Bordeaux has fallen to your enemy, and a governor he has set over your fief now does his will there—"

Hearing this, Huon did give an exceedingly bitter cry and held out his hands beseechingly to the messenger. But the bright one had no mercy upon him yet. For when he asked:

"Claramonde and the little one, how fares it with them?"

The messenger made answer: "Your daughter was borne to Cluny by the Squire Bernard and there bides safely with the Abbot, your uncle. But your lady wife lies prisoner in the dungeon tower of Mayence and piteous is her lot. Worse still shall be her fate if you return not to succor her."

Now Huon stood upon his two feet and from his eyes flashed the fire of dire anger and his right hand crooked to the sword hilt.

"Go you forth, Huon of Bordeaux, to the edge of this garden, and there you shall find a boat floating upon a river. This will bear you hence so that you may come again to save those who have trusted in you. These only may you take with you—"

The Being stretched out his hand, and at his light touch three of the apples parted from their stems and fell to the ground, rolling to Huon's feet.

"These be the Apples of Eternal Youth and whosoever eateth of them shall never again feel the touch of age, but shall ever be young in the pride of his best youth. Guard them well for they shall serve you in the days to come."

So having spoken, the Being disappeared and Huon stood alone with the Apples of Youth at his feet. But now his heart was heavy with care and sorrow for those he loved and he had no wish to remain in that garden. Returning to the fountain he put on again his mail and fastened his sword belt about him and donned his helm. Then, with the apples bound within a corner of his surcoat and the griffin's limb within his hand, he crossed the garden and came in time to a stream whereupon rested a small boat.

Very curiously fashioned of ivory and ebony was this boat, so that half of it was black and half white. And within it were cushions of the finest damask and silk from the East which even a king might have been proud to wear upon his body.

Huon pushed the boat off from the shore and took the tiller, letting the current bear him where it would, with the faith in his heart that he would again see Bordeaux.

All day the stream bore him swiftly along and he broke his fast with the viands and drink he found stored in boxes and flagons at his feet. But his mind was not at ease and, had he been able, he would have quickened that voyaging a hundredfold.

Now the stream began to run between high rock walls and in time these met far overhead to form a roof lost in the shadows. So Huon knew that he had been carried underground. But it grew no darker and he perceived that light arose out of the water itself, and, after a while, having no fear, he laid him down and slept.

In that hour he dreamed that he saw the Lady Claramonde encompassed in gray stone and black iron and that her fair face was white and wan and that she stretched forth her hands and cried out to him for aid. But he was held apart from her by some force so that he could reply not.

Struggling, he awoke to find that beneath him the boat rocked and that he was still underground, but was moving not. And for the first time since entering upon the stream he was afraid, afraid that he might be trapped there underground with no hope of reaching light and day once more.

XI. HOW HUON VOYAGED UNDERGROUND AND MET WITH THE FAITHFUL BERNARD ONCE MORE

BY THE LIGHT which came from out of the water he saw that the prow of his boat had struck into a bar of sand and gravel which thrust out into the stream. And he leaped out upon this to see what damage his vessel had suffered. In the gravel under his feet lay divers stones which glowed and blazed with fiery light and by the aid of these he perceived that the boat had taken no harm from the mishap, but was merely caught.

Wishing to have more light with him in this place of lasting gloom he scooped up from the sand these glowing gems and tossed them into the boat where they made a glittering heap like unto a sea lantern for light. Then, putting his shoulder to the boat, he pushed it off into deep water once more and jumped aboard as the current gripped it and carried it on.

For another space of time he ate and slept within the dark, but when he awoke for the second time he found himself on an open bay of the sea and saw in the distance the walls and towers and wharves of a city. Then did he raise the sail which lay within the boat and the wind bore him toward that city where many flags and banners hung from the battlements as if those within celebrated some feast day.

Huon's boat came in to one of the wharves and the people there marveled to see so small a ship fashioned in so rich a manner. They called out to Huon, asking who he was and from whence he came. Thus did he learn in talk with these sailors that this was the city of Tauris in the land of Persia and that the Shah of the land abode now within its walls, having proclaimed a feast for all comers in honor of the Lord Jesu, the Shah having but recently become a Christian.

Then did Huon give thanks aloud that he had come to a Christian land and he decided to go before the Shah and pray aid of him. But, before he stood in the palace of the ruler of Persia, a great and joyous happening was to befall him and in this manner.

After the Squire Bernard had taken Clarette to Cluny and left the child safe there with the Abbot he bethought himself that he must now search out his lord, the Duke Huon, wherever in the world he might be, and bring him the dire tidings of what had chanced in Bordeaux. So he took ship and sailed to the eastern seas upon that quest.

First came he into the port of Jaffa where he went among the Knights of the Cross and all manner of traveling merchants and far-voyaging sailors, asking for news of his lord. But no man there had heard aught of Huon. From Jaffa, Bernard next went to Jerusalem, but here was no news either. So finally he made the journey to Cairo, and long and perilous that journey was. There, when he was asking through the merchants' quarters for tidings of far-off lands, he met a Frankish trader who replied to him thus:

"Friend, but lately I have heard that the Shah of Persia has been newly converted to belief in our faith. And for the honor of this faith he has proclaimed a feast to be held in his city of Tauris for all comers. Merchants will go thither to trade their wares, and surely in such a gathering you will gain some news of your lord. I, myself, am fitting out a caravan to travel to Tauris and, if you wish, you may travel with me."

It seemed to Bernard that this was sage and excellent council. Accordingly he joined with the Frankish merchant across the desert into the fields of Persia, coming in good time to the city of Tauris. There he did go down to the seaside, planning to ask news of the sailors new come to that port. And there was hope in his heart, for many strange ships lay at anchor there—so many that their masts were as a forest of trees.

By chance he came to the very wharf where Huon had tied up his boat, and there Bernard heard of the coming of the foreign knight who had appeared so strangely out of the sea. He went on board the boat hoping that this stranger might have some word of his master. And there he saw Huon, but since the Duke was fully armed and helmed he saw not his face nor knew that here stood the very man he sought.

But Huon, knowing him, cried out a loud and joyful greeting:

"Bernard of Bordeaux!"

And the Squire replied: "In truth here stands Bernard once of that unhappy city. But you, sir, I know not."

Straightway Huon put up the visor of his helm so that his face was uncovered to the day and Bernard, with a shout of thankfulness, fell down upon his knees and gave glory to Our Lord for bringing him so to his journey's end after such weary searching. Then he made known unto the Duke how ill had chanced matters since Huon had left his city.

But Huon, having already heard this tale from the Being in the garden, was not so stricken and said unto his faithful squire:

"Good youth, we have stout arms and swords—and with these, God willing, we shall put right what is wrong. Now we must find gold to take us back to France—"

But Bernard, while his lord had been speaking, noted a strong light coming from out a coffer on the deck before him. And now he asked what lay within. Huon replied that it contained certain stones he had found in the sands of the underground river and he told to Bernard the full tale of his wanderings.

The squire opened the coffer and, when he saw what lay within, he was greatly astounded and cried:

"Now here lies one of the greatest treasures that is in our world. For these be the lost jewels of the Elfmen and of them I have heard many a tale and of them I have read many a time in the ancient chronicles. It is said that these jewels do turn night into day, and in addition they have other virtues."

Out of the pile he took an amethyst of purple as deep as the robes of state.

"Now the property of this is that he who wears it cannot be poisoned, nay, not even if his cup brims with venom, and he may also pass through fire and water without any hurt.

"While the wearer of this"—and Bernard brought forth a diamond which was like unto a star for frozen brilliance—

"cannot hunger or thirst, nor does his countenance show the ravages of time, man's eternal enemy.

"This emerald heals the wounds of him who bears it and restores the sight of those blinded, if it be laid upon their eyes. While this ruby conquers all ills of the body. With it upon you, you need not fear even the Black Plague. And also it will eat away the chains of any prisoner, if touched to the iron, and last of all it can render its wearer invisible at his will.

"Fifth and last be this carbuncle which will light for you the darkest night, and if you bear it into battle no foe man can touch you.

"These five be the lost stones of Elfland. And a mighty treasure they are. Sell these if you will, lord"—he pointed to the rest of the gems which lay within the coffer still—"but keep the mystic five, I pray you!"

"Fear not—that I shall!" Huon replied, joyful for his great good fortune.

XII. HOW HUON GAINED THE GOOD WILL OF THE SHAH AND MARCHED TO FREE THE HOLY LAND

HUON AND BERNARD went into the city of Tauris together and even into the inner court of the Shah who was greatly astonished to see a Frankish knight and squire so far from their native land. But he received Huon and his follower with much courtesy, urging that they join in the feasting. And, when they had stayed their hunger, he had Huon brought before him again and asked the Duke why he had come so far from the realm of France. Then Huon made full answer, telling all that had befallen him during the year just past.

The Shah was moved by his story, so that he said unto Huon:

"Lord Duke, many and grievous have been the trials of heart and body which have been laid upon you. Were I in my youth again, then would I go out into the Holy Land in your company so that we might walk together, where the feet of Our Lord Jesu have trod, and fight righteously for Him, putting to the sword all infidels and devil worshipers who now hold that land. Thus having so wrought in His Name and cleansed me of all sin, I would sail across the seas with you and ride out against this traitor emperor who has so despitefully used you and yours."

Huon thanked the Shah for his kind words, saying in reply:

"Lord, my heart rejoiceth much in what you have said. For to free the Holy Land from the impious hands of the infidel is indeed a good and glorious task, and if I strive to do this as best I can then surely will Our Lord Jesu further my efforts to free again Bordeaux."

He then untied the corner of his surcoat and took therefrom the Apples of Paradise which had lain amongst its folds. And these glowed so it seemed that the sun itself had been loosed there in that room. One of the fruits he laid before the Shah who took it up, amazed at its beauty and fragrance.

With a smile Huon said, "Eat of this fruit, Lord Shah, and all that you have wished for shall be possible—"

Then did the Shah bite deep into the fruit so that the juice of it ran out upon his white beard and age-trembling hands. But, lo, as he ate, his back grew straight again, his beard and hair darkened, and he was as a man in the full prime of his youth. And he and all of his court cried aloud their astonishment at this, demanding of Huon whence came this marvelous fruit. So that Huon answered them with the tale of the Apples of Paradise and the shining Being he had seen within the garden of that place.

Also did he give unto the Shah certain jewels he had taken from the underground river, but not those which were of Elfland, and into his hands he offered also the boat which had borne him to Tauris. And all wondered at the richness of these gifts.

But Bernard took the magic gems to a worker in gold and jewels and had them set into a sword belt which Huon wore about his body, nor did he again part from that, since he trusted in the strange properties of the stones.

Out over all his land did the Shah then send the summons for his warriors to assemble. And in not too long a time he had gathered an army such as even the Emperor of Alamayne could not boast of leading. One half of this force he placed under the command of Huon and he himself rode in the van of the other half. So they marched into the Holy Land.

There they took the city of Angore after much hard fighting and they put to flight a vast rabble of Saracens and infidels. But from Angore they needs must take ship upon the sea to reach their next goal. And storm clouds gathered black overhead so that these ships took refuge in the lee of a mountain which arose from the sea.

Huon, looking closely upon the crown of the mountain, thought that from its peak he might well see the course of the storm and whether or no it would keep them long pent within the bay. So, despite the pleading of his men, he set out to climb to that point.

Now the top of the mountain was flat and square and naught was there save a huge tun, or cask, of iron-bound wood. And by this tun lay an iron mallet of no small size or weight. From the tun issued forth all the while the voice of a man weeping and wailing.

Huon advanced to the tun and rapped upon it with his fist, calling out to know what manner of prisoner lay within it. And a voice returned answer, saying:

"If you be mortal man then you have come in good time to save me. Know you that I am that Cain who struck down his brother in hot anger. And for that fault I have been sealed in this place to bide until the end of measured time. But if a mortal man takes up the mallet which lies beyond and strikes in the head of this foul prison, then may I issue forth and join with the demons of the underworld which it is my fond wish to do. Nor will you be able to depart again from this place unless you so serve me!"

Huon went from the tun to the edge of the mountain slope and looked down into the bay. Thus he saw that the ships, and his men within them, were being driven by the wind and storm out into the sea so that he was left alone behind. And he returned again to the tun and called out:

"Holla, Cain, you say that there be a way out of this place. Tell me of it and I shall do as you wish. The mallet is within my hand even now." And he struck upon the rock with the mallet so that the iron rang loud.

"Free me first," began Cain, but Huon laughed aloud as he replied:

"Nay. For I cannot trust you in any part. Speak first, or I shall serve myself as best I can."

And Cain, fearing that Huon would do even as he said, answered quickly:

"On the sea below awaits a ship manned by a demon. When I am free and go below I have only to show to him the mallet which now you hold and he will ferry me across the sea in safety to wherever I wish."

When he had heard these words Huon tapped lightly upon the tun and said:

"Many thanks to you, Cain. Now will I go to prove the truth of that story."

"Free me!" shouted Cain.

"Not so. For if you have been so set in your prison by the Will of Our Lord, it is not meet that man should free you until the proper time."

Then did Cain roar out his rage, and in his anger he made plain his own black heart for he screamed:

"Had you loosed me as I asked, then would I have rent you limb from limb, for my hate against all men is hot!"

"So do I believe," replied Huon. And with the mallet in his hand he went down again from that mountain place.

XIII. HOW HUON WAS FERRIED BY A DEMON ACROSS THE SEA AND AFTERWARDS DREAMED AN OMINOUS DREAM

WHEN HUON CAME down from the mountain top, the path he followed led im into a narrow cove wherein was moored a boat as red as the fires of Hell, with sails as black as the nights of sin. and the master of this craft was a fearsome demon of so monstrous a face and form that Huon was fain to turn away his eyes, lest the sight breed in him real terror.

This demon, sighting the Duke, shouted forth in a loud and roaring voice, which brought stones tumbling down the cliffs above them:

"Ha, Cain, and is it you yourself? A thousand thousand years have I waited here for your coming. Now show me speedily the sign agreed upon and I shall set you across the sea that you may be able to work all manner of ill in the world of mortals!"

And Huon, rejoicing within him that he had not freed Cain, not only to his own undoing but to the sorrow of the world of men, spoke no word in return, only raised on high the mallet he carried and stepped aboard the ship.

Straightway the demon cast off the lashings which held the craft fast and took the tiller in his taloned hand. Out of nowhere there arose a wind which filled their darksome sails and bore them out to sea, carrying them on a course through the waves. All night they voyaged thus, speaking no word one to the other. And in the morning, so swift had been that sailing, Huon saw before them a fair harbor in which lay a multitude of ships at anchor. His heart leaped high as he knew by the banners upon them that these were of the fleet of the Shah from which he had been lost.

Turning to the demon, he spoke for the first time.

"Set me ashore upon yonder spit of sand for here be gathered a mighty army of mankind and amongst them I may cause all manner of mischief and dire trouble."

Hearing him, the demon laughed aloud and smote his hands upon his hairy thighs for the pleasure he took in such words. And he obeyed readily, steering for the spit of sand reaching out into the sea, saying, twixt roars of evil mirth:

"Verily will you serve our master well, O Cain. I shall carry good report of you to him in Hell. But tarry not too long at this sweet business of bringing men to death and ruin, for there is other work awaiting you."

Huon leaped ashore, and the demon and ship were gone in an instant, leaving him alone by the sea. So he walked along the strand until he came to the camp of the Shah. And there he was made welcome with great joy and wonder, which grew with every word of the story he had to tell.

After his coming, they did take this city of Colander which the army of the Shah had held in siege, and many and great were the deeds of valor done in that taking—chief among them being the feats of arms performed by Huon. Dread of him grew among the enemy so that whole companies took flight from the field and rode away in disorder before the passage of the Shah's forces.

Thus did they march in triumph to Antioch, Damascus and at last reached Jerusalem, where Huon bowed himself at the Tomb of Our Lord and prayed for the success of his arms in the field and a safe return to Bordeaux and the relief of the grievous troubles there.

Now in the plains beyond Jerusalem the Saracens gathered all their armies into one, determined to fly no longer but to meet the foe in one last battle. And to the Emir who was the commander there came the Giant Dorbrye. Taller than any two men of that company was he and tusked were his jaws, as are the jaws of the wild boar that lives in the deeps of the forest. His sword was the length of a man and his shield as high as a city gate. The steed he rode was horned like unto a bull and when it breathed it puffed forth flame and smoke.

This Giant claimed of the Emir the right to meet Huon in single combat and the Emir granted him that right. So when the battle began Dorbrye rode fiercely into the fray seeking the Duke, and with each sweep of his sword he slew man or horse.

So terrible was this battle that the sun was darkened by the flight of arrows overhead, and the dust—torn up by the hooves of the mounts—made worse the murk so that the day was as twilight.

In this mist Dorbrye at last found Huon and, before the Duke could move, he slew Huon's horse with one stroke and took the French knight up with one hand, throwing him across his own saddle before him. So did Huon think that his hour of death had come at last, and he prayed aloud for help against the dire fate which lay before him. But Dorbrye's horse, coming into a place where many dead lay thick upon the ground, stumbled and fell, and both the Giant and Huon were thrown from the saddle.

Huon won to his feet first and, before Dorbrye could rise, the Duke aimed a shrewd blow at his bare throat and so killed him. Then Huon mounted upon the Giant's horse and rode back to the fighting. Thereafter none could touch him by reason of his great skill at arms and the belt of magic gems which he wore.

At last the Saracen army fled the field and the men of Persia were left victorious. They pitched their tents by a river and that night feasted their fill, taking much pleasure in it.

In the morning they followed the fleeing Saracens, even to the walls of Acre where the Emir took refuge—sending messengers this way and that across all the infidel lands asking for aid. Several of these messengers fell into the hands of the Persians and having heard the tidings they bore, Huon said to the Shah:

"My lord, by the Eternal Grace of Our Lord Jesu, we have done many mighty deeds, freeing much of the Holy Land from the rule of the unbeliever. But in the doing of this we have lost many men and the land of Persia lies far away, so we can hope for no aid from there. But this Emir has sent messages far and near asking for help against us and if he is fitly answered by only a portion of those who hear him, then shall we be ground to dust between the millstones of our enemies. Therefore it will be wise to hold what we have taken and not be greedy in seeking more."

All those in the presence of the Shah raised up their voices in support of this advice and at last the Persian ruler agreed that it was right.

But that night Huon dreamed a dark and awesome dream. For as in a vision he stood on the wide plain without the walls of a mighty city. Here was erected a pyre for the burning of some criminal. And, as he watched, out of the city came a procession bearing the victim to be burned. But, lo, it was not a criminal they threatened with so cruel a death but his own fair lady!

He awoke from that dream with a cry of horror and despair and ran straightway unto the Shah and told him of that vision, saying that he must return to France with all speed lest that horrid dream prove true.

The Shah wept sorrowfully at their parting, but he gave unto Huon seasoned men-at-arms and a great treasure and he wished him well under the power of God. So did Huon and Bernard take ship once more for their native land, but there was no rejoicing in their hearts—only fear.

XIV. OF CLARAMONDE AND HER GREAT DANGER

OVER THE CITY of Bordeaux reigned the governor the Emperor had placed there, and for a full year had he held that office. Heavy were the burdens he put upon that proud city so that men ofttimes remembered their Duke Huon and his gentle lady and in their hearts they hated the Emperor with a black and ever growing hate. There were still those amongst them who had once served in the Duke's household and who had fought right valiantly in the defense of the city. And now these did band together and secretly plot that they would, when the hour was right, strike boldly for their freedom.

But in their midst was a traitor and he disclosed all their

plot unto the governor. So, in the night, armed men surrounded the dwelling places of those who had dared to hope for better days. And all these were speedily seized and taken before the governor, to be as quickly judged and sent out of the city in chains for the long and weary march to Mayence with only the gallows and a rope to think of as their future.

Now the Abbot of Cluny—he who was fond uncle to Huon and the protector of Huon's daughter—heard of this happening. And straightway he summoned to him those knights who owed service to the Abbey. These he bade lead out their men and ambush the Emperor's party to free those who were being marched to their deaths.

And it all chanced as the Abbot had hoped. The Emperor's men were routed and put to utter defeat, and their commander, a baron of the Emperor's own household, was killed. But the men of Bordeaux were set free and came to Cluny to claim protection of the Abbot, making many plans against that day when they could enter again into their city with triumph.

When the news of this defeat came to the Emperor his wrath waxed so hot that his words strangeled in his throat and he choked upon them until he could shout:

"These men of Bordeaux be very devils for stubbornness. While any of Huon's house live so will they continue to hold against me, rising up again and again. Therefore shall I make an end to this—for Huon himself be surely dead over the sea or he would have returned long since slavering for my blood as a hound in chase.

"So let the Duchess Claramonde be taken beyond the city walls and there let her be burnt after the manner of a traitoress and let all those from Bordeaux who lie within our ward be hung at that same time!"

And no man among all his court could turn him from this purpose or soften his words.

Thus beyond the city walls was built a tall pyre of seasoned wood, even as Huon had seen in his evil dream, and by this was erected a forest of gallows trees to hold those of Bordeaux who had been forced to yield them when the city fell.

On the appointed day the Lady Claramonde and her people were brought out of prison to face this cruel fate. So pitiful was the lady and those who followed her that the people of Mayence raised loud their voices and cried out against their rightful lord, the Emperor, saying that no good would ever thereafter come to that city or the land where such a foul deed was done, nor would he who so ordered it afterwards prosper. They closed their doors and windows and bode inside their houses in darkness and sorrow, praying for the souls of those about to perish.

Now it chanced that the Duke Hildebert, who was now the Emperor's heir, rode into Mayence at that hour and he saw the men of Bordeaux, with their Duchess at their head, on foot and in chains being led to their deaths. And he asked concerning this matter. When the truth was told to him he was sore stricken with pity and horror, and, setting spurs to his horse, he rode furiously to where the Emperor was waiting and called aloud to him:

"My good lord, I pray you in the Name of the Lord Jesu, do not do this thing. For, if by your orders this sweet lady and these people of Bordeaux die so, then will your name be remembered with loathing by all men. If your quarrel lies with the Duke Huon, then pursue it with him and not with helpless women and prisoners surrendered to your mercy. For only to the merciful will true mercy be granted!"

But so blinded and held by the power of his great hatred was the Emperor that he was as flint to the pleading of Hildebert, and his answer came cold and bitter:

"My lord Duke, you forget to whom you now speak. If you do not bridle your foolish tongue it may lead you into some such an end as these traitors are now facing."

And when Hildebert would have protested again his own friends surrounded him and bore him struggling away, lest the Emperor make good that threat.

Then were the people of Bordeaux, knight and commoner alike, put upon the gallows and around their throats were

placed the hempen loops. While the Lady Claramonde was made fast to the stake and the brands heaped about her.

At that same hour King Oberon was holding high revel for his kinswoman, the peerless Morgan le Fay, and all was joy within his halls—save that only Oberon himself sat with a bowed head and sad countenance, until at last the Lady Morgan said unto him:

"How now, fair cousin. Here is all joyful feasting and fine frolic and yet you sit alone in sorrow and silence. Why do you thus?"

Oberon made her answer in a low and melancholy voice.

"Sweet cousin, above all my kin and friends here within the borders of our own magic land do I love Huon, Duke of Bordeaux. By my sworn promise is he my heir, to rule after me in these halls until the end of mortal time. But because of this I am bound by our laws not to aid him, since he must win here by his own efforts. And now behold what happens to the one he holds dearest in all the world!"

He moved his hands across a mirror which hung on the wall of the hall. The glass misted and when it again cleared it showed to those who were with him the plain before the walls of Mayence and what chanced there. Then did the Elf knights Gloriant and Malabron arise in their places and go unto Oberon, kneeling before him in supplication. And Malabron spoke for the twain of them when he said:

"Lord King, true by the laws of this land you may not stretch forth your hand or power to now rescue this lady. But we be not bound by that. And though our power be not a tenth or a hundredth part of yours, it is more than any mortal can stand against. Let us go and succor the Duchess Claramonde!"

With the shadow of hope upon him Oberon consented and those two disappeared from before him.

So, as Claramonde stood watching with fearful eyes the burning brand that the executioner bore toward her, there appeared in the sky above Mayence a flash of unearthly fire and out of the heart of this sprang the Elf knights fully armed and ready for war.

By their power the chains fell in dust from those of

Bordeaux and the men of Mayence were stricken blind so that, when they were able to see once more, Claramonde and her people stood unharmed and free, giving thanks to the Most High for their deliverance.

And even the Emperor was disturbed in his mind so that he ordered the prisoners taken back to the dungeons, but spoke no more against them.

XV. OF HUON'S RETURN TO FRANCE AND HIS APPEARANCE AT THE COURT OF THE EMPEROR

HUON RETURNED secretly to France and journeyed with his men to the Abbey of Cluny, letting no one know of his coming. The Abbot marveled at his safe arrival, for he had long mourned him as one dead, and now he ordered that those in the Abbey should give thanks to God for this good happening and that a feast be made for Huon and those who followed him.

Then did the Abbot also send for the baby Clarette to be brought unto her father, and greatly did Huon rejoice upon seeing his daughter and give humble thanks unto his uncle for his exceedingly good care of her. And the Duke brought in a chest of rare gems and pieces of gold which was a portion of the spoil gained in fighting the Saracens and which he now settled upon his daughter as a dowry. And about her neck he placed a fine necklace of rubies set cunningly in gold, and he gave rich gifts to the lady who nursed her.

Having been so pleased with looking upon his daughter once more, he turned again to the Abbot with these words:

"Dear kinsman, my heart is full and runneth over with good will toward you for the way you have served my daughter. If there is aught which I may do for you in return, speak it aloud in this hour."

The Abbot smiled upon him, but there was a faint shadow of sadness in his voice as he made answer.

"Nay, fair son and kinsman, there is naught in the power

of man to grant me which I now desire. Within the walls of Cluny is my world and it is a good one. That which I might wish for is beyond your power of attainment. For look you, I am an old man, much worn by the years and no one can bring me youth and strength again. Winter and age have twisted these old bones and wasted the flesh from my limbs. Who can turn that season into spring once more?"

Then did Huon's eyes shine with happiness and he hurried to the chamber given to him and from his most precious possessions he brought forth the second of the Apples of Paradise. This he set before his uncle, urging him to eat thereof and speedily.

Wondering at the strange manner of his nephew, the Abbot did as he was bid. Now as he ate a strange thing came to pass. No longer did he seem an old man bent by time and frosted by age. But he sat straight and tall, once more a man in the pride of his youth, and all those within the chamber were struck dumb by this miracle. Then did Huon relate how these apples had come into his hands and all the rest of the long tale of his wanderings.

Having seen his daughter, the Duke now planned to go into Mayence where he might, with the aid of the Lord Jesu, set free those who believed and trusted in him, the chiefest being the Lady Claramonde for whom his heart hungered with a pain which never ceased.

So did he take the juice of nutshells and brown his face and hands and let loose his hair to hang untidily upon his shoulders. He put off his bright mail, leaving on him only the belt of wondrous gems. And this he did conceal under the worn clothes of a pilgrim and a shabby cloak of the hue of beaten ashes, so that he seemed one who might beg his way from door to door.

And Bernard did likewise so that no man would know him. In this guise they went into Mayence, arriving there at Eastertide. The city was full of pilgrims who had come thither to visit a shrine, and from these pilgrims Huon learned two pieces of news which were worth much to him.

The first was that when the Eastertide be over the Emperor had sworn a most solemn oath before all his lords that

he would do to death all those from Bordeaux and with
them the Lady Claramonde. And this made Huon's heart cold
within him. Bernard urged that he go again to Cluny and
bring to Mayence those who were Huon's men that they
might make a desperate sortie to free their lady from this
dire peril.

But Huon said him nay for he thought upon the second
thing he had heard and there seemed to lie within that the
germ of hope.

"Long have we been at war," he said unto Bernard, "and
many men have we slain. But these were unbelievers and
not of our race and kin. If we go up against the Emperor
now with bared swords and the harness of battle girt upon
us, more innocent blood will flow, all to no man's gain. Still
your hot blood and list now to me. It is the custom of this
Emperor to go to mass early upon the Easter morn and
when the mass is said and done he will grant to the first
asking it of him any boon that man desires, swearing to that
on the high altar itself.

"Now it is in my mind to go into the church in the early
hours of this night and seek out a place close to where the
Emperor shall be. And if God will it so, that first boon shall
be mine. The Emperor dare not gainsay it afterward, lest he
be forsworn before the eyes of all Christendom!"

So Huon did as he had planned. He put on him again
the robe of a belted knight, but he did not order his hair or
wash the stain from his flesh. And over this robe he pulled
the beggar's cloak. Then he went into the cathedral and
took a place not far from where the Emperor would stand.
So did he bide the remainder of the night, praying for success in his venture.

In the very early morning the Emperor and his court
came to hear mass and few noted the beggar who stood in
the shadow, but when the mass began Huon took from beneath his cloak a rosary. And this rosary was made of fine
gold and the beads of it were carved gems, the cross wrought
ivory. And the Emperor, loving such treasures, saw enough
of it to wish to see more. So when the mass was done he

moved not from his place but beckoned Huon to approach him.

"Whence had you that treasure, pilgrim?" he asked.

"From far lands, Lord Emperor, even from the hand of the Holy Father in Rome." Huon held closer the rosary and the Emperor feasted his eyes upon it and coveted it greatly.

Then did the Duke stake his all upon one chance and he said:

"Lord Emperor, the men of Mayence have told me that on this Easter morn you do grant to the first asker of it the boon of whatever he wishes. Be this the truth?"

The Emperor, surprised, replied, "Pilgrim, it is the truth."

"Then do I claim that boon, Lord Emperor!" And Huon's voice was no longer that of a humble pilgrim but rang with all the pride of his blood and youth.

"It is thine, be what it may," returned the Emperor slowly, for he sensed that more lay behind this than was clear to ear or eye.

"Free the Lady Claramonde and those of Bordeaux who lie within your power and with me swear friendship and eternal peace!"

The Emperor started back and his face was as bleak as winter as he demanded:

"Rash man, who are you to ask such a thing of me?"

Then did Huon drop the beggar's cloak and shake back his hair. Though the dark stain was still upon him he was so comely that all with the Emperor marveled at him and believed him surely a prince of the blood royal. And he said, in his clear and ringing voice:

"I be Huon, Duke of Bordeaux!"

XVI. HOW HUON MADE PEACE WITH THE EMPEROR AND RECEIVED THE MESSENGER OF OBERON

So ASTOUNDED was the Emperor that he could speak not a word in that instant and, when again his voice came to him, he remembered the oath he had sworn and that he must give this upstart Duke the boon he asked of him. But before he could answer, Huon fell upon his knees before him and said:

"Much blood has been shed by the twain of us, Lord Emperor. But know you—I have spent this year in misery and despair. And in the Holy Land I fought to free the Tomb of Our Lord from the defilement of the infidel and there did I pray for the forgiveness of my sins. Therefore I beseech you most humbly—let there now be peace between us and let us swear friendship before this holy altar on the Day of the Ressurection of our dear Lord and Master."

Then did the stone which had walled up the heart of the Emperor crack and his frown was not so black. So Huon, taking heart, continued:

"Liege man was I from birth to the King of France. But in the hour of my greatest need he came not to my succor, nor did he send even one man-at-arms to my service. Therefore do I now declare that my fealty to him is at an end and that I owe him allegiance no longer. But Bordeaux is no large fief, able to stand alone. So do I now make petition unto you, Sire, to take it as a fief of your crown and let me serve you for it!"

Now was the heart of the Emperor truly moved and he put his hands over Huon's and took him as his liege man, raising him up to his feet and bestowing upon him the kiss of peace. So did all there rejoice, knowing that strife and unhappiness had come to an end at that moment.

The Emperor decreed a feast and to it came all those of Bordeaux who had so long lain prisoners in his dungeons. Not the least of these was the Duchess Claramonde. And when Huon received her again into his arms he wept with joy and gave thanks aloud for this favor from Heaven.

From the inner pocket of his cloak he then took the third and last of the Apples of Paradise and this he laid in a dish of fair silver before the Emperor. The apple glowed with golden light and from it arose such a sweet savor it was as if musk and spices had been burned in the hall. Then the Duke of Bordeaux related to the company the story of the fruit and when he had done the Emperor did eat of it. His hair of gray darkened again and his face became plump and ruddy, so that once more he was in his comely youth. All his lords and knights cried aloud in wonderment at the sight and the Emperor had such joy as he had never known before. So as Huon and his people departed to their own city, they went with the love and good will of all the nation of Alamayne.

Once more in Bordeaux, the city and those released from prison rejoiced at their freedom. And Huon, his lady, and their daughter dwelt in great peace and happiness. But not for long was this to be.

For at nighttime on a certain day of the dying year a knight with a fair train of followers rode into Bordeaux. No man had marked the manner of their coming, they seemed to have sprung from the earth itself. And they stayed not until they came into the hall of the castle.

Having heard of this knight, Huon came forth to greet him courteously, and, as the knight raised the visor of his helmet, he looked upon and knew that it was Malabron of the Elf realm whom he had known beforetimes.

But the face of Malabron was sad and tired and Huon mistrusted what message he might bring. He led him to the upper table and offered him meat and drink. But Malabron refused, saying:

"Lord Duke, my liege lord—the King Oberon—has sent me hither with this message. It is close now upon that time when he must go out of Elfland into Paradise as was foretold at his birth. Therefore he commands you and your lady to come unto him speedily that he may give into your hands the rule of his kingdom before he departs therefrom—"

Huon bowed his head and answered:

"Sir knight, I accept the command laid upon me by your dread lord and master. Let me but know the way that I must follow to come unto his land and that I shall travel."

And Malabron replied:

"Get you and your lady down to the sea on the second morn from this, and there you shall find a ship awaiting you. It will bear you to the boundaries of our kingdom. But delay not, for our master is weary and impatient to depart."

Having so delivered his message Malabron and those with him vanished out of the hall as if they had never been. Then did Huon summon unto him the Abbot of Cluny and Bernard. And he told them of the message from Oberon which he dare not disobey. And he ended in this wise:

"Since my kingdom will not be of this mortal earth I shall no longer walk among men nor sit here in the castle of Bordeaux. But my daughter Clarette is heir of my house and of my duchy and to your care do I entrust her. Keep her safe and guard well her inheritance until she comes to womanhood. See that the lord she weds is in all ways worthy of her so that she will be ever happy and blest!"

The Abbot of Cluny and Bernard were full sad at hearing these words and they longed for Huon to remain with them. But they knew that by the will of Oberon he had no choice.

Many tears did the Lady Claramonde shed as she kissed her daughter and bade her farewell. Also she said unto her lord:

"Elfland is truly not of this earth but the longing of a mother's heart may well bridge the gulf which lies between. I do not think that I now say good-bye to this, my daughter, for all time."

Then did she put into the hands of the Abbot her chest of jewels and order him to hold these until the maiden be of years to delight in their wearing. And she summoned all her women and bade them have special care of her daughter.

Thus did Huon and Claramonde make ready to depart out of Bordeaux for the last time.

XVII. HOW HUON AND CLARAMONDE SAILED FOR OBERON'S KINGDOM AND OF THEIR ADVENTURE WITH THE WHITE MONKS

IN THE DAWN of the next day Huon and his lady bade farewell to Bordeaux and all those within its gates whom they loved with all their hearts, and Claramonde said unto her husband:

"My dear lord, save that this was your home where you were born and brought to man's estate, I have little love for this city, for here have our sufferings been greater than our joys. But it is in my mind that Clarette shall be happier in this place than we have been, so do I go hence with a lighter heart."

And she laid her hand upon the hand of Huon right joyfully and alone they went down unto the shore of the sea. There, even as Malabron had foretold, was a ship fashioned of all the fragrant woods of the East. And the nails which held the wood were of gold and silver, and the sails of fine silk, green in color after the uses of Elfland.

No captain trode the deck nor was there any crew on board to bid them welcome. But when they were safely upon her the sails arose without hands to bend them and the ship sped out into the ocean, as they watched the walls and towers of Bordeaux grow less and less behind them.

So for three days they were borne across the waves of the western ocean without danger or mishap. All manner of dainty food and drink was to be found and silk-hung couches awaited their slumbers. For the first day, the Lady Claramonde and Huon thought often, and with some sadness, of those left behind and spoke of them together. But as the time sped as easily as the waves of the sea they thought more and more of what would be their life in the days to come and they wondered as to what would be their fate in the strange Elfland which lay beyond the borders of the world known to mortal man.

On the fourth day they saw before them land, lying as a dark cloud upon the water, and almost at sunset the ship came into a small harbor where its anchor fell so that they knew that the voyage had come to an end. But as the night was almost upon them, the Lady Claramonde did not wish to leave the safety of the ship for the unknown shore where there seemed to be no manner of habitation.

Even as she hesitated there sounded clear on the evening air the tolling of a bell, such as might grace some church or abbey. And Huon, smiling, said:

"Dear heart, list to that and have no more fear within you. For that be one of the signals of Christendom and if we are guided by it we shall reach good shelter."

So heartened, she followed him from the ship and they went inland from the sea until on the far side of a hill they came upon a fair abbey set in wide green fields as a peerless gem is set in gold. As they came to the gate the bell left off its calling, but a multitude of doves wheeled across the sky and vanished beyond the wall.

When Huon rapped upon the wicket it was flung wide, and there stood a monk clad all in robes of purest white, who said to them:

"Enter, my children. Blessed be Our Lord for bringing you hither to shelter within our walls and give us opportunity to serve God's creatures, for few come this way and we have but scant chance to practice Christian charity."

Huon and Claramonde were brought into the guest house of the abbey and there received with great courtesy, such as might be granted a king and queen. Thus, because their hearts were thankful for all the favors the Lord had shown them, they arose at midnight to attend mass.

But, lo, when the service was but half completed the monks left their places and filed from the chapel. Now did Huon seize upon the last one in the line, holding him by the full sleeve of his habit, and he cried:

"Sir monk, why mock you thus Our Lord, saying but half the mass?"

The monk tried in vain to pull free, making no answer. But Huon held tight and with his other hand he made the sign of the cross saying:

"By this blessed sign do I command you to answer me—what manner of monk be you and why is your mass broken?"

When Huon made the sign the monk shivered through all his body as if he were suddenly lapped by a chill wind. But he raised up his head and with his two hands he folded back his cowl so that they could look directly upon his face.

And, behold, it was dark and sad and not like the visage of mortal man, for there dwelt on his brow such sorrow as no one born of this world could bear and live. Seeing this Huon dropped his hold upon the other's sleeve and he asked for the third time:

"Who are you—man or demon? Or be you one of the dwellers within the boundaries of Elfland?"

And now the monk made answer saying: "Neither man, nor demon, nor of the Fairy are we. Not of Elfland, or Hell, or of Earth. We are those who once stood in the ranks of Heaven. And when proud Lucifer made rebellion against Our Lord we did not take up the sword to him, but neither did we join those who strove with the hosts of angels. Therefore we were sent out of Heaven to this land which is on the border between the mortal world and that which lies beyond the world of men, but which is neither above nor below it. And here we must bide until the Day of Judgment. If then we can stand forth cleanly, without sin, but with pride to praise Our Lord with joyful hearts, then we may enter in again to our lost home. But the weary waiting is like a brand laid upon us and we have naught but everlasting regret to company us through endless time!"

Once more did Huon make the sign between them. And when he spoke, his voice was softened by pity.

"If the prayers of mortals may aid you, then know that we twain shall evermore remember you in ours. Friend, let there be peace between us."

And a single tear dropped from the eye of the monk as he nodded twice his head.

"Your words shall be for us as rain is for the sun-parched land. Fain would we keep you with us, but this half land is not for such as you. Behind you lies the mortal world and before you Elfland. Whither would you go?"

Huon took Claramonde by the hand as he made answer:

"This be my wife, the Lady Claramonde, and I am Huon, once Duke of Bordeaux in the realm of France. But now we are under the command of the King Oberon to journey into Elfland where he is minded to render unto us the rule of that country."

When he had heard this the monk bowed low.

"Fair lord and lady, greatly are we honored by your coming among us. At the breaking of the dawn I myself shall lead you to that point from which you may pass into your own domain."

So when the rose dawn light was in the sky the monk led them forth from the White Abbey and between two green hills. And there before them lay a pleasant and smiling land wherefrom arose the tall towers of castles and the glittering walls of stout cities. Fairer than any they had ever seen was that land. But the monk would not look upon it. Rather did he cover his face with his two hands as he said:

"Go forth into your own place and prosper there. Before you lies now the land you seek."

And as Huon and Claramonde went down into that green and golden land there sounded in the air the trumpets of a mighty host as would hail the coming of great and worthy souls.

XVIII. HOW HUON AND CLARAMONDE WERE GREETED BY OBERON AND CAME INTO THEIR KINGDOM

THUS WERE THESE two welcomed into their land and they came to the castle where Oberon was. Now when he saw them enter his hall he arose in great joy and came forward to them. And each he embraced and kissed in greeting, saying:

"Dear friends, now do I rest content, for you have fulfilled the promise made long ago and have come hither to take from me the heavy burden of kingship, so that I may go hence and rest in Paradise. Now shall I summon unto this court all those who owe service and loyalty to me so that they may swear the same unto you."

And he took Huon and Claramonde to the top of the highest tower in that keep and from a bow of ebony and gold he loosed four arrows, north, east, south and west. As these flew through the air they gave forth a marvelous trilling which was the summons of the High King of Elfland.

Then in answer to that there gathered from the four corners of that land a diverse and wondrous company. From the mountains came dwarfs and kobolds, goblins and air sprites. From out of the streams sprang merpeople and nixies and the green kelpies. From the fires darted forth the glowing sala-manders and dragons, and out of the green earth came the elves and will-o'-wisps, nymphs and fauns.

To all these did Oberon speak of his going, and they sorrowed, for long had he ruled them and just and wise in all ways had been that rule. Then he brought forward Huon and Claramonde, and all those gathered there did swear to them fealty and all loyalty.

But when this was done there came another into that hall, behind him a train of armed warriors. And this was that Arthur who had once reigned in Britain and for many years had dwelt thereafter in Avalon between the worlds. And he reproached Oberon with these words:

"How this, King Oberon? If you choose to go out of your kingdom, that is your right, which no man will gainsay you. But why have you summoned this mortal, who is but a green youth, to rule in your place? Elfland needs a strong hand over it and that hand be mine!"

And those who had accompanied him echoed that claim. But Oberon only shook his head and replied:

"It is true that the laws made by men do not run in this land and our ways are not their ways. But still are we subject to certain decisions which may not be altered. Upon my first meeting with this Huon it was made plain to me that it was he who was ordained to follow me upon this throne. So are we all bound—"

But the countenance of Arthur was red with wrath and he broke in upon the words of Oberon.

"I, who was King in Britain, shall not be second in this other world. Let this youth beware of me if he dares to lay any commands upon me or mine!"

On hearing this Oberon, too, lost his serenity and he replied hotly:

"Not yet has my power departed from me. So I say unto you, Arthur, be not so rash in provoking my wrath. For it is in my mind to lay a doom upon you. Persist in this rebellion and you shall return to the mortal world a ravening creature. Man by day and wolf by night. And all shall hate and fear you until your miserable death."

But Huon dared then to put out his hand and touch the clenched fist of Oberon. And he said:

"Lord Kings, both of you be mighty men and powerful lords. Raise not your anger against one another over this matter. All men knoweth the worth of Arthur of Britain. Who be I to take what is his?"

Oberon smiled then upon Huon, and he thought for a moment before turning to Arthur with these words:

"This other world be very great. No one, even I, knows its true boundaries. And beyond it lies that evil which is always pressing against the lands of light. It is the duty of him who rules here to be ever on his guard against the blackness—to be at eternal war with the evil from beyond. Therefore I give unto you, Arthur, the marches of the East, to hold with all your strength and spirit. And to you, Huon, I give the wardenship of the West, and you shall both king it in this world with no dispute between you."

Then did Huon and Arthur clasp hands in good friendship and swear upon their honor that it should be as Oberon had decided.

So did Oberon put off his crown and sword and all the trappings of his kingship, and he blessed his people there assembled to do him honor. Then he kissed first Claramonde with the kiss of peace, and then Huon and Arthur. Alone did he walk down that hall, all making a clear path before him and when he came nigh unto that great window which formed one end of the room, there shone in through it a bar of light, which was gold and silver, and all the colors of Heaven and earth intermingled. And from this bar of light, which seemed to those watching like unto a gate, there came the sound of wondrous singing.

Oberon looked upon those of his court for the last time. And he smiled full sweetly. Then he stepped through this gate of Paradise and was gone from them.

Since the world of Elfland no longer borders so close upon the world of mortals, having slipped somewhat awry in time and space, no man truly knows what now chances therein. But rumor says that Huon holds well the marches of the West against those evil things which breed in the dark to trouble the souls of men and that this valiant war never ceases nor shall until the Day of Judgment. With the face of fair youth and the wisdom of age he and his lady reign in Elfland to the greater good of all mankind.

And this be the story of Huon, once Duke of Bordeaux, the end of it being unknown to this very hour.